MAFEKING ROAD
and other stories

THE ANNIVERSARY EDITION OF HERMAN CHARLES BOSMAN

Planning began in late 1997 – the fiftieth anniversary of Bosman's first collection in book form, Mafeking Road – *to re-edit his works in their original, unabridged and uncensored texts. The project should be completed by 2005 – the centenary of his birth.*

GENERAL EDITORS:

STEPHEN GRAY AND CRAIG MACKENZIE

Herman Charles Bosman

MAFEKING ROAD
and other stories

The Anniversary Edition

Edited by Craig MacKenzie

Human & Rousseau
Cape Town Pretoria Johannesburg

Copyright © 1998 by The estate of Herman Charles Bosman
First published by Human & Rousseau in 1969
Anniversary edition published in 1998
Second impression 1999
Human & Rousseau (Pty) Ltd
Design Centre, 179 Loop Street, Cape Town

Back cover photograph of Herman Charles Bosman in Johannesburg,
canvassing adverts for *The S. A. Opinion*, late 1940s, taken by a street
photographer, courtesy of the Harry Ransom Humanities Research Center.

Cover design by Robert Meas
Typography by Welma Odendaal
Typeset in 11/13 pt Times New Roman
Printed and bound by National Book Printers
Drukkery Street, Goodwood, Western Cape

ISBN 0 7981 3902 1

HERMAN Charles Bosman was born near Cape Town in 1905, but spent most of his life in the Transvaal. In 1926 he was posted as a young teacher to a farm school near Zwingli in the Marico District of what was then the Western Transvaal. This position was abruptly terminated after he was arrested and convicted for the murder of his stepbrother during a vacation at the family home in Johannesburg; he spent nearly four years in gaol after his death sentence was commuted to life imprisonment.

After his release on parole in 1930 he worked as a journalist in Johannesburg before leaving for London in 1934, where he was to spend the next six years. It was in London that he wrote the bulk of the stories that constitute *Mafeking Road*. He died suddenly of a heart attack in 1951, having seen only three of his works into print: *Jacaranda in the Night* (1947), *Mafeking Road* (1947) and *Cold Stone Jug* (1949), his prison memoir.

Mafeking Road was an instant success and quickly became one of South Africa's best-loved works. The text has always been printed replete with numerous errors, however, something that Bosman himself noted but was never able to correct.

This edition attempts to restore the text as far as possible to the version Bosman intended.

Contents

Introduction

FIFTY years or so ago, when Herman Charles Bosman (1905-51) saw his first collection of short stories into print – *Mafeking Road*, the only one that would appear during his lifetime – he brought to fruition a dream he had cherished for some time. As early as 1932 he had approached the Central News Agency with the view to publishing a selection of his stories in book form, but had been turned down. Yet in late 1946, by which time he had published in magazines over thirty of his Oom Schalk stories, Bosman was himself approached by the CNA with the same idea.

In a letter that has only recently seen print as part of some correspondence between Bosman and Roy Campbell (in *English in Africa*, May, 1997), Bosman recounts the event:

You can imagine what I felt. I was unable to speak. I had actually thought I was too old to care, anymore. I collected together such stories as I could lay my hands on. But I was in such a hurry to get the book out that I didn't do what I had always intended: i.e., to restore them as far as possible to the way they were originally, when I wrote them. Many details in the book have offended, quite a number of them. The result is that pieces of it were cut as if for reasons of space. Various editors also inflicted emendations of their own. Consequently, my stories in *Mafeking Road* now only appear in mutilated form. In the end, perhaps the picture is not much affected. But I am acutely conscious of this.

This brings me to the matter of your kind offer to help me find an English publisher. In spite of the foregoing, and thanks to my long wait with the CNA, you will realise that if you would do that for me it would make me extremely happy. I am deeply indebted to you already, however. Nevertheless, I trust that you will appreciate that it is because I am *very* keen on finding an English publisher – and not because I am conscienceless in regard to accepting favours – that I accept your offer most gratefully.

As it happened, nothing came of Campbell's attempt to find Bosman a British publisher, although he did arrange for several of the *Mafeking Road* stories to be broadcast on the BBC. Two years later Bosman was dead, and *Mafeking Road* was left to steer its own course through the numerous editions and impressions since 1947 which have made it an all-time bestselling South African classic.

If Bosman was privately aggrieved at the "mutilated form" in which *Mafeking Road* appeared, the South African public did not seem to notice. "One of the best things to have happened in South Africa for many a day," Mary Morison Webster opened her review in the Johannesburg *Sunday Times* (on 14 December, 1947). "Bosman's stories are nothing if not poetry," averred Edward Davis in *Trek* (in January, 1948). Even the *Times Literary Supplement* ran a notice (on 14 February, 1948): "Mr H. C. Bosman's stories of the South African veld have an individual flavour; some are extremely funny. . . all are good." And it must have been this notice which prompted Campbell to write to Bosman "just to say that I think your stories in *Mafeking Road* are the best that ever came out of South Africa" – a puff that has been quoted on the jacket ever since. Other early and vocal admirers included F. D. Sinclair, Oliver Walker, Anthony Delius and William Plomer.

MAFEKING ROAD

by

Herman Charles Bosman

Cover of the first edition (1947) of *Mafeking Road*. Illustration by Wilfrid Cross, first used for "Starlight on the Veld", *The South African Opinion*, 10 January, 1936

The rapturous reception accorded *Mafeking Road* was not a passing fad. Since 1947 no fewer than six editions of the text have appeared and many thousands of copies sold. The popular Dassie paperback edition succeeded the first CNA hardback and went into six impressions between 1949 and 1963, when the CNA put it back into hardback. Human and Rousseau began issuing Bosman's works in their uniform edition in the 1960s, their *Mafeking Road* appearing in hardback in this series in 1969. This edition went into fourteen impressions up to 1987 before being reset in 1991. *Mafeking Road* has also been included in Bosman's *Collected Works*, which appeared in two different editions in 1981 and 1988.

Individual stories from *Mafeking Road* have been reprinted in several selections of Bosman's work and in many anthologies of South African stories over the years. Perhaps the most reproduced is "The Rooinek", which David Wright chose to open his Faber anthology of 1960, *South African Stories*, and which has been translated into German, Danish, Hungarian, French…

What has been the effect of the errors made in *Mafeking Road* in the 1947 and 1949 editions and mostly carried through to the present? The short answer is, very slight. Indeed, casual readers of this new edition of *Mafeking Road* will probably notice few changes; Bosman was therefore probably correct in observing to Campbell: "In the end, perhaps the picture is not much affected."

None the less, following strictly professional standards, the carelessness with which the text has been treated is shocking. In quantitative terms, between fifty and a hundred errors have been allowed to persist in the various editions, all of which have been corrected here. In addition, some forty to sixty new words have had to be introduced in order to restore the stories to their original form. (The exact figures vary according to the edition one consults.) Readers who are very familiar with the old text will notice a few new sentences and phrases here, and also perhaps find greater consistency in spelling and punctuation. The overall effect of these corrections is subtle and cumulative, and it is in order to set the record straight that this new edition of *Mafeking Road* has at last been undertaken. (A full account of the textual history of the stories and the editorial measures adopted is provided in the notes at the end.)

It is well known by now that in January, 1926, Bosman was sent as a novice teacher to a one-room, Afrikaans-medium school on the farm Heimweeberg near the tiny trading-post of Zwingli in the Groot Marico District, in what was in those days the Western Transvaal. His stay was brief, but the impression the region and its people made on the young man was lasting: nearly all of his 150 short stories are set in the Marico, and over fifty of them make use of the storyteller figure, Oom Schalk Lourens.

Oom Schalk was uprooted from the Free State and settled there as a farmer, not at the present hamlet of Groot Marico, but in the far north of the district, across the Dwarsberg range with its sentinel of Abjaterskop, near Derdepoort on the border of the then Bechuanaland Protectorate. After the devastation of the Second Anglo-Boer War (symbolised in the title story and described so vividly in "The Rooinek"), he and his neighbours were allocated concessions there, up the road from Nietverdiend, under the administrative and religious centre of the increasingly British town of Zeerust. This was a buffer zone between British high commission territory with its missionary road and railway to the north, and the densely populated Tswana territory (which would in the 1970s become the part of Bophuthatswana with Mafikeng as its centre) to the east of the Marico River.

Oom Schalk we must imagine is living in what is technically the Georgian period (of King George V, post-Union in 1910), although his memory stretches back through the reigns of Edward and Queen Victoria to the first murder trial ever held in the Transvaal, not yet unified under President Kruger's Volksraad, at its then southern capital at Potchefstroom (as in "The Widow"). Incredibly, Oom Schalk as a youth even went on the commando extermination campaign against Chief Makhapane of the Tlou people in 1854, after Hermanus Potgieter and his party were killed by Chief Mapela, one of Makhapane's allies; Kruger himself took part in that action, a mere stripling of twenty-nine. Although Bosman is scrupulously accurate on frontier history – on the original Thirstland Trek, re-enacted in "The Rooinek", there even was a character called Webber (actually Weber) – Oom Schalk's own biography does not bear too much scrutiny. Not for nothing was he called the greatest liar that ever trekked.

The Marico District he knows so intimately is not only Bushveld, but the real Backveld or Gramadoelas. Bosman's characters are not so

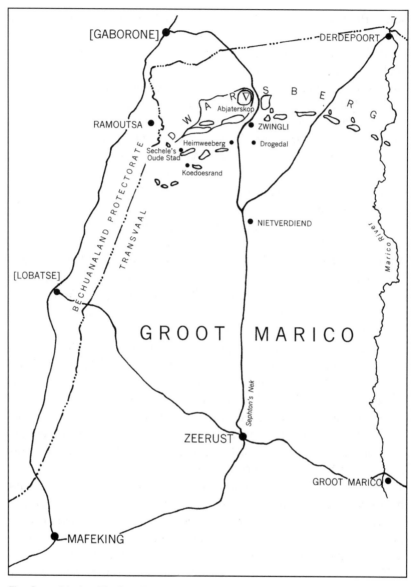

The Groot Marico District, circa 1920

much Boers even, but Takhaars, as one would expect from the difficult and poverty-stricken conditions in which they find themselves. Their natural enemies are the local tribespeople with whom they are in deadlock over grazing and water, as over the border the Bechuana retain their transhumant and economically successful cattle-posting ways. Although there is much jesting about this, they have also had devastating epidemics like the rinderpest to deal with, locust invasions to demolish their staple mealie-lands (which Oom Schalk wants the painter's canvas to deflect in "Veld Maiden"), and droughts so recurrent and critical that Oom Schalk's community is still able to think of inspanning and trekking off as a solution (north to the Limpopo, as in "Starlight on the Veld"; or north-west towards German and Portuguese territory, as in "The Rooinek"). Only a generation before freebooters had declared themselves independent from even the Transvaal – at Vryburg and Schweizer-Reneke there was the refuge of the Stellaland Republic. They still shoot game routinely to supplement their farm produce, and are professionals at illicitly distilling the fruits of the bush into mampoers. Coffee they make locally, too – when they cannot afford to buy it from the traders at Ramoutsa.

Their poverty is gently exposed in their homemade veldskoens, worn without socks, and they still gather by candlelight, they still smear cattle-dung on their floors. Their way of life is easily threatened by the commercial world on which they depend for trek-chains and borehole-pumps; they are pushovers for smouses or tinkers bringing new gadgets, like a thermometer or a gramophone, or some other novelty like an insurance policy. The government of Pretoria is but dimly represented by tax-collectors and the odd pair of mounted policemen. The rich mining world of Johannesburg, which provides a market for beef (either their own or that smuggled from across the border), and where black men walk on the pavements reading newspapers, is even more distant – although not too distant to lure young Bushvelders seeking the glamour and employment the Marico cannot provide.

The railway may have reached Zeerust, but Oom Schalk's people still ride about on mule-carts like poor whites. To challenge their isolation they have the weekly post-cart to look forward to, and then that phases into the government lorry. Broadcasting is not yet a medium of news and entertainment (as it is in the later Voorkamer stories) – these characters are still in the age of the tickey-draai and concertina-con-

14

cert. The bioscope is eating away at the edge of their isolation, however, and Oom Schalk has twice bunked Nagmaal in Zeerust to sample this forbidden fruit. Sensing its threat, he stubbornly resists the kind of modernisation it represents, by insisting – and often proving – that the oldest stories are indeed the best.

Despite his bluff appearance, he is never caught out when it comes to the ultimate truths of basic human motivations (often shocking lusts, rivalries, trade-offs and killings). In order to blend in with his surroundings he must present himself as a rather addled old duffer, only marginally more artful than his sometimes dismally inarticulate audiences, but this is merely a guise behind which his astute understanding of human nature is free to roam. Ever alert to hypocrisy, he shows in "The Prophet" how a false white prophet is unmasked by a true black one – in the process demonstrating that the techniques of verbal persuasion are not copyrighted by any one race. He himself is in danger of being unseated only when that Indian shopkeeper sets up in competition as a more exotic decorator of narratives in the crucial story with which Bosman chose, as his ars poetica, to conclude his selection.

Illustration of "The Prophet" by Wilfrid Cross, *The S. A. Opinion*, December, 1945

Nor is Oom Schalk's own storytelling ever merely folksy. He folds one tale into another in the best style, is the master of ellipsis (knowing "what part of the story to leave out"), and in the most polished fashion practises all the other techniques he lists in the title story as necessary parts of the formula. Having spent a good deal of his time in the voorkamer and around the camp-fire, he knows that it is often not so much the story that counts, but how you tell it. Time and again, he is so skilful at constructing a work that Bosman has him reach across to us and catch us out, too. Bosman saw to it that the old backveld raconteurs he learnt so to admire would continue to be preserved as they always were: true spellbinders. About the verbal arts, as Oom Schalk himself said, he did know a thing or two.

Bosman was heir to a venerable tradition of yarnspinning that stretches back to the South African hunting tale of the mid-nineteenth century, which he knew, admired and collected. In A. W. Drayson's *Tales at the Outspan* (1862), for example, we encounter a series of stories told around the camp-fire by locals and travellers from abroad who have come to hunt Africa's teeming game. In one of these tales a leopard makes an appearance, the hunter recounting his hair-raising escape. Drayson's work may be superficial and ephemeral – little more than an attempt to evoke Africa for his metropolitan readers by way of a simple tale of adventure – but Bosman sees its potential and in a story like "In the Withaak's Shade" turns it into an occasion for far more.

Drayson had more artful successors – Ernest Glanville, Perceval Gibbon and Francis Carey Slater among them – who all used first-person narrators in a way that set these figures up for the joint amusement of author and reader. A prototype of Oom Schalk Lourens occurs in Slater's stories about 'Oom Meihaas', a takhaar Boer who is both indolent and an eloquent teller of tall tales. Glanville's 'Abe Pike' character, although English-speaking and from the Eastern Cape frontier, is even closer to Oom Schalk Lourens in his deceptive complexity. And Gibbon's 'Vrouw Grobelaar', for her part, has the raconteur's gift for artful verbal exchange; casual and desultory conversation on the stoep during the evening leisure hours usually prompts the Vrouw to call forth a moral or two and illustrate it by telling a tale. J. Percy FitzPatrick, Eugène Marais and Sanni Metelerkamp all had a go at working up this South African way of recounting wild and woolly experience.

Bosman took this 'oral-style story' on to a different plane. He introduced tightness into the narrative structure, and thereby perfected it. Whereas Glanville, Gibbon and Slater all rather clumsily used first-person frame-narrators who are present at the storytelling event and who then satirically 'relay' the story to the reader, Bosman collapses these functions into his one figure. Oom Schalk is therefore both a comic character and a skilful narrator, a backveld bumpkin and a far-sighted sage. In him is invested all the complexity and 'double-voicedness' that was latent, and largely dormant, in the earlier works.

Cover of the first number of *The Touleier* by H.E. Winder

By 1930, when Oom Schalk made his debut in "Makapan's Caves", the fireside tale had outlived its usefulness as an 'authentic' mode of representing South African life. It was now capable only of yielding a kind of deluded nostalgia for the frontier era or, on the other hand, of offering a conventional foil for the operation of unconventional, disruptive devices. It is of course the latter possibility that is exploited so richly by Bosman: he takes over many of the features of the oral tale – a narrator, a conversational narrative style, an appropriate milieu and an implied audience – but he introduces to it elements which are among the hallmarks of the modern literary short story – economy, irony, structural tautness and social critique.

Bosman was also the inheritor of an international tradition of the English-language short story, which he always acknowledged, celebrated and turned to his own purposes. Although he used a boisterous yokel as his mouthpiece, this was only to cover his tracks as an erudite and studious practitioner of his craft. Often he paid tribute to Edgar Allan Poe, one of the founding fathers of the American short story, for his Gothic allegories – "The Gramophone" and "Drieka and the Moon" are his attempts at making tales of the grotesque. A case can be made for "In the Withaak's Shade" being a reworking of an African story by the French romantic Honoré de Balzac, "A Passion in the Desert" (1832), available in South Africa in English translation in various school readers. In "Willem Prinsloo's Peach Brandy" he rearranges Olive Schreiner's "The Woman's Rose" (1893), which is all about the limited number of flowers and finishing school young ladies available to a surfeit of hickish rural swains.

The later nineteenth-century humorists whom Bosman so enjoyed are nudging influences as well. For example,

> I can't sit still and see another man slaving and working. I want to get up and superintend, and walk around with my hands in my pockets, and tell him what to do. It is my energetic nature. I can't help it.

This off-hand circumlocution is not Oom Schalk's, but Jerome K. Jerome's (in *Three Men in a Boat*, 1889). In the fiercely ironic "Splendours from Ramoutsa", the contest in storytelling we see may be between that Indian trader and Oom Schalk, but behind them the

Sanskrit *Mahabharata* is being debunked by Mark Twain.

O. Henry, whom Bosman admired and so resembled, is there, particularly in the technique of twisting and turning the plot with hair-trigger inflections to a snapper ending. As Stephen Leacock noted in his 1919 essay, "The Amazing Genius of O. Henry", the trick as a plot-maker is to keep the reader in suspense until the very close, and then to "turn on the lights and the whole tale is revealed as an entirety." From W. W. Jacobs, whom Bosman interviewed during his London years, he learnt the potential of real-life comedy delivered in vernacular monologues.

Popular culture of the day also contributed, especially as regards women in those silent Hollywood films who had learnt not only to achieve equality with men, but in melodramatic love-triangles to exert a god-like power over them. Hence Drieka the sultry vamp, the wispy temptress Marie Rossouw in "Mampoer" who had kissed Satan, and Sannie the faithless wife – portrayed rather nakedly as a whiff of aesthetic smoke in "Veld Maiden" – who has her long-haired art student win out. In "Ox-wagons on Trek" the bandit horseman and demon lover is playing the role of Rudolph Valentino (in *The Sheik* of 1926).

In-jokes abound as well, played straight-facedly without winking. "The Gramophone" is a repeat of one of Bosman's own sketches of his fellow convict, the murderer whom he named 'Rosser', who once he had killed his wife, buried her under the living-room floor. (This is in turn arguably a reworking of a motif in "The Tell-tale Heart" (1845), the Poe horror story about a deranged man who kills his tenant and buries him under the floorboards of his bedroom.) In "The Widow" Tjaart van Rensburg is a sly self-portrait of the young Bosman – a good-looking prisoner in handcuffs, wearing his hat like a lady's man at a saucy slant, on trial for murder and proudly proclaiming his guilt. And all those digs from Oom Schalk about green school-teachers being sent out to tame the Marico.

With his crony and publisher, Aegidius Jean Blignaut, there was much leg-pulling as well:

Schalk Lourens? Yes, I know him. He has blue eyes and a long beard. I used to go to the Dwarsberg to tell him stories, true stories. . .

Thus Blignaut's Hottentot Ruiter in "The Camp Fire" (in *The New*

Sjambok, 31 August, 1931). For Bosman fiction was some vast inherited text to be continually revised and redesigned to his own ends.

The Marico where Oom Schalk's wiseman's talents were so successful has recently disappeared forever. Already it was going in "The Music Maker", the one story Bosman chose for his own anthology of the best of South African work, *Veld-trails and Pavements* (1949), which describes the drift. Now in a corner of the new South Africa's North West Province, the Marico has proved largely unsustainable as agricultural settlement and is partly dammed up for its north-flowing river to provide the new Botswanan capital of Gaborone with water. To serve the tourist industry it has become South Africa's fourth-largest game reserve, the Madikwe, with its luxury lodges on the restocked plains. Leopards (like the famous one of "In the Withaak's Shade") may have been threatened with extinction in the old days, but have since been reintroduced. Worst of all, moonshine stills have now become ecologically sensitive – and legal.

The lost schoolhouse in those wild hills, where Bosman was sent by the Transvaal Education Department in its wisdom to subvert the Afrikaner oral tradition of his forefathers with the chalky alphabet and the letter of the English text, in effect turned him around. Those canny speeches at the local Debating Society at Drogevlei, those tactical discussions with parents whom he learnt to call Oom and Tannie, over refreshments on their stoeps, taught him what his formal education had not: the art of eloquence. In all his years in exile in London at the heart of the motherland, where all but five of these stories were written, he would keep rebelling against the regime of print, never forgetting the lessons taught him at its farthest, most deprived fringe.

Stephen Gray and Craig MacKenzie
Johannesburg, 1998

Starlight on the Veld

I T was a cold night (Oom Schalk Lourens said), the stars shone with that frosty sort of light that you see on the wet grass some mornings, when you forget that it is winter, and you get up early, by mistake. The wind was like a girl sobbing out her story of betrayal to the stars.

Jan Ockerse and I had been to Derdepoort by donkey-cart. We came back in the evening. And Jan Ockerse told me of a road round the foot of a koppie that would be a short cut back to Drogevlei. Thus it was that we were sitting on the veld, close to the fire, waiting for the morning. We would then be able to ask a kaffir to tell us a short cut back to the foot of that koppie.

"But I know that it was the right road," Jan Ockerse insisted, flinging another armful of wood on the fire.

"Then it must have been the wrong koppie," I answered, "or the wrong donkey-cart. Unless you also want me to believe that I am at this moment sitting at home, in my voorkamer."

The light from the flames danced frostily on the spokes of a cartwheel, and I was glad to think that Jan Ockerse must be feeling as cold as I was.

"It is a funny sort of night," Jan Ockerse said, "and I am very miserable and hungry."

I was glad of that, too. I had begun to fear that he was enjoying himself.

"Do you know how high up the stars are?" Jan asked me next.

"No, not from here," I said, "but I worked it all out once, when I had a pencil. That was on the Highveld, though. But from where we are now, in the Lowveld, the stars are further away. You can see that they look smaller, too."

"Yes, I expect so," Jan Ockerse answered, "but a school-teacher told me a different thing in the bar at Zeerust. He said that the stargazers work out how far away a star is by the number of years that it takes them to find it in their telescopes. This school-teacher dipped his finger in the brandy and drew a lot of pictures and things on the bar counter, to show me how it was done. But one part of his drawings always dried up on the counter before he had finished doing the other part with his finger. He said that was the worst of that dry sort of brandy. Yet he didn't finish his explanations, because the barmaid came and wiped it all off with a rag. Then the school-teacher told me to come with him and he would use the blackboard in the other classroom. But the barmaid wouldn't allow us to take our glasses into the private bar, and the school-teacher fell down just about then, too."

"He seems to be one of that new kind of school-teacher," I said, "the kind that teaches the children that the earth turns round the sun. I am surprised they didn't sack him."

"Yes," Jan Ockerse answered, "they did."

I was glad to hear that also.

It seemed that there was a waterhole near where we were outspanned. For a couple of jackals started howling mournfully. Jan Ockerse jumped up and piled more wood on the fire.

"I don't like those wild animal noises," he said.

"They are only jackals, Jan," I said.

"I know," he answered, "but I was thinking of our donkeys. I don't want our donkeys to get frightened."

Suddenly a deep growl came to us from out of the dark bush. And it didn't sound a particularly mournful growl, either. Jan Ockerse worked very fast then with the wood.

"Perhaps it will be even better if we make two fires, and lie down between them," Jan Ockerse said, "our donkeys will feel less frightened if they see that you and I are safe. You know how a donkey's mind works."

The light of the fire shone dimly on the skeletons of the tall trees that the white ants had eaten, and we soon had two fires going. By the time that the second deep roar from the bush reached us, I had made an even bigger fire than Jan Ockerse, for the sake of the donkeys.

Afterwards it got quiet again. There was only the stirring of the wind in the thorn branches, and the rustling movement of things that you hear in the Bushveld at night.

Jan Ockerse lay on his back and put his hands under his head, and once more looked up at the stars.

"I have heard that these stars are worlds, just like ours," he said, "and that they have got people living on them, even."

"I don't think they would be good for growing mealies on, though," I answered, "they look too high up. Like the rante of the Sneeuberge, in the Cape. But I suppose they would make quite a good horse and cattle country. That's the trouble with these low-lying districts, like the Marico and the Waterberg: there is too much horse-sickness and tsetse-fly here."

"And butterflies," Jan Ockerse said sleepily, "with gold wings."

I also fell asleep shortly afterwards. And when I woke up again the fires were almost dead. I got up and fetched more wood. It took me quite a while to wake Jan Ockerse, though. Because the veldskoens I was wearing were the wrong kind, and had soft toes. Eventually he sat up and rubbed his eyes; and he said, of course, that he had been lying awake all night. What made him so certain that he had not been asleep, he said, was that he was imagining all the time that he was chasing bluebottles amongst the stars.

"And I would have caught up with them, too," he added, "only a queer sort of thing happened to me, while I was jumping from one star to another. It was almost as though somebody was kicking me."

Jan Ockerse looked at me in a suspicious kind of way.

So I told him that it was easy to see that he had been dreaming.

When the fires were piled high with wood, Jan Ockerse again said that it was a funny night, and once more started talking about the stars.

"What do you think sailors do at sea, Schalk," he said, "if they don't know the way and there aren't any other ships around from whom they can ask?"

"They have got it all written down on a piece of paper with a lot of red and blue on it," I answered, "and there are black lines that show you the way from Cape Town to St. Helena. And figures to tell you how many miles down the ship will go if it sinks. I went to St. Helena during the Boer War. You can live in a ship just like an ox-wagon. Only, a ship isn't so comfortable, of course. And it is further between outspans."

"I heard, somewhere, that sailors find their way by the stars," Jan Ockerse said, "I wonder what people want to tell me things like that for."

He lay silent for a while, looking up at the stars and thinking.

"I remember one night when I stood on Annie Steyn's stoep and spoke to her about the stars," Jan Ockerse said, later. "I was going to trek with the cattle to the Limpopo because of the drought. I told Annie that I would be away until the rains came, and I told her that every night, when I was gone, she had to look at a certain star and think of me. I showed her which star. Those three stars there, that are close together in a straight line. She had to remember me by the middle one, I said. But Annie explained that Willem Mostert, who had trekked to the Limpopo about a week before, had already picked that middle star for her to remember him by. So I said, all right, the top star would do. But Annie said that one already belonged to Stoffel Brink. In the end I agreed that she could remember me by the bottom star, and Annie was still saying that she would look at the lower one of those three stars every night and think of me, when her father, who seemed to have been listening behind the door, came on to the stoep and said: 'What about cloudy nights?' in what he supposed was a clever sort of way."

"What happened then?" I asked Jan Ockerse.

"Annie was very annoyed," he replied, "she told her father that he was always spoiling things. She told him that he wasn't a bit funny, really, especially as I was the third young man to whom he had said the same thing. She said that no matter how foolish a young man might be, her father had no right to make jokes like that in front of him. It was good to hear the way that Annie stood up for me. Anyway, what followed was a long story. I came across Willem Mostert and Stoffel Brink by the Limpopo. And we remained together there for several months. And it must have been an unusual sight for a stranger to see three young men sitting round the camp-fire, every night, looking up at the stars. We got friendly, after a while, and when the rains came the three of us trekked back to the Marico. And I found, then, that Annie's father had been right. About the cloudy nights, I mean. For I understood that it was on just such a sort of night that Annie had run off to Johannesburg with a bywoner who was going to look for work on the mines."

Jan Ockerse sighed and returned to his thinking.

But with all the time that we had spent in talking and sleeping, most of the night had slipped away. We kept only one fire going now, and Jan Ockerse and I took turns in putting on the wood. It gets very cold just before dawn, and we were both shivering.

"Anyway," Jan Ockerse said after a while, "now you know why I am interested in stars. I was a young man when this happened. And I have told very few people about it. About seventeen people, I should say. The others wouldn't listen. But always, on a clear night, when I see

26

those three bright stars in a row, I look for a long time at that lowest star, and there seems to be something very friendly about the way it shines. It seems to be my star, and its light is different from the light of the other stars. . . and you know, Schalk, Annie Steyn had such red lips. And such long, soft hair, Schalk. And there was that smile of hers."

Afterwards the stars grew pale and we started rounding up the donkeys and got ready to go. And I wondered what Annie Steyn would have thought of it, if she had known that during all those years there was this man, looking up at the stars on nights when the sky was clear, and dreaming about her lips and her hair and her smile. But as soon as I reflected about it, I knew what the answer was, also. Of course, Annie Steyn would think nothing of Jan Ockerse. Nothing at all.

And, no doubt, Annie Steyn was right.

But it was strange to think that we had passed a whole night in talking about the stars. And I did not know, until then, that it was all on account of a love story of long ago.

We climbed on to the cart and set off to look for the way home.

"I know that school-teacher in the Zeerust bar was all wrong," Jan Ockerse said, finally, "when he tried to explain how far away the stars are. The lower one of those three stars – ah, it has just faded – is very near to me. Yes, it is very near."

Willem Prinsloo's Peach Brandy

N
o (Oom Schalk Lourens said) you don't get flowers in the Groot Marico. It is not a bad district for mealies, and I once grew quite good onions in a small garden I made next to the dam. But what you can really call flowers are rare things here. Perhaps it's the heat. Or the drought.

Yet whenever I talk about flowers, I think of Willem Prinsloo's farm on Abjaterskop, where the dance was, and I think of Fritz Pretorius, sitting pale and sick by the roadside, and I think of the white rose that I wore in my hat, jauntily. But most of all I think of Grieta.

If you walk over my farm to the hoogte, and look towards the northwest, you can see Abjaterskop behind the ridge of the Dwarsberge. People will tell you that there are ghosts on Abjaterskop, and that it was once the home of witches. I can believe that. I was at Abjaterskop only once. That was many years ago. And I never went there again. Still, it wasn't the ghosts that kept me away; nor was it the witches.

Grieta Prinsloo was due to come back from the finishing school at Zeerust, where she had gone to learn English manners and dictation and other high-class subjects. Therefore Willem Prinsloo, her father, arranged a big dance on his farm at Abjaterskop to celebrate Grieta's return.

I was invited to the party. So was Fritz Pretorius. So was every white person in the district, from Derdepoort to Ramoutsa. What was more, practically everybody went. Of course, we were all somewhat nervous about meeting Grieta. With all the superior things she had learnt at the finishing school, we wouldn't be able to talk to her in a chatty sort of way, just as though she were an ordinary Boer girl. But what fetched us all to Abjaterskop in the end was our knowledge that Willem Prinsloo made the best peach brandy in the district.

Fritz Pretorius spoke to me of the difficulty brought about by Grieta's learning.

"Yes, jong," he said, "I am feeling pretty shaky about talking to her, I can tell you. I have been rubbing up my education a bit, though. Yesterday I took out my old slate that I last used when I left school seventeen years ago, and I did a few sums. I did some addition and subtraction. I tried a little multiplication, too. But I have forgotten how it is done."

I told Fritz that I would have liked to have helped him, but I had never learnt as far as multiplication.

The day of the dance arrived. The post-cart bearing Grieta to her father's house passed through Drogedal in the morning. In the afternoon I got dressed. I wore a black jacket, fawn trousers, and a pink shirt. I also put on the brown boots that I had bought about a year before, and that I had never had occasion to wear. For I would have looked silly walking about the farm in a pair of shop boots when every-body else wore homemade veldskoens.

I believed, as I got on my horse, and set off down the Government Road, with my hat rakishly on one side, that I would be easily the best-dressed young man at that dance.

It was getting on towards sunset when I arrived at the foot of Abjaterskop, which I had to skirt in order to reach Willem Prinsloo's farm, nestling in a hollow behind the hills. I felt, as I rode, that it was stupid for a man to live in a part that was reputed to be haunted. The trees grew taller and denser, as they always do on rising ground. And they also got a lot darker.

All over the place were queer, heavy shadows. I didn't like the look of them. I remembered stories I had heard of the witches of Abjaterskop, and what they did to travellers who lost their way in the dark. It seemed an easy thing to lose your way among those tall trees. Accordingly, I spurred my horse on to a gallop, to get out of this gloomy region as quickly as possible. After all, a horse is sensitive about things like ghosts and witches, and it was my duty to see my horse was not frightened unnecessarily. Especially as a cold wind sud-denly sprang up through the poort, and once or twice it sounded as though an evil voice were calling my name. I started riding fast then. But a few moments later I looked round and realised the position. It was Fritz Pretorius galloping along behind me.

"What was your hurry?" Fritz asked when I had slowed down to allow his overtaking me.

"I wished to get through those trees before it was too dark," I answered, "I didn't want my horse to get frightened."

"I suppose that's why you were riding with your arms round his neck," Fritz observed, "to soothe him."

I did not reply. But what I did notice was that Fritz was also very stylishly dressed. True, I beat him as far as shirt and boots went, but he was dressed in a new grey suit, with his socks pulled up over the bottoms of his trousers. He also had a handkerchief which he ostentatiously took out of his pocket several times.

Of course, I couldn't be jealous of a person like Fritz Pretorius. I was only annoyed at the thought that he was making himself ridiculous by going to a party with an outlandish thing like a handkerchief.

We arrived at Willem Prinsloo's house. There were so many ox-wagons drawn up on the veld that the place looked like a laager. Prinsloo met us at the door.

"Go right through, kêrels," he said, "the dancing is in the voorhuis. The peach brandy is in the kitchen."

Although the voorhuis was big it was so crowded as to make it almost impossible to dance. But it was not as crowded as the kitchen. Nor was the music in the voorhuis – which was provided by a number of men with guitars and concertinas – as loud as the music in the kitchen, where there was no band, but each man sang for himself.

We knew from these signs that the party was a success.

When I had been in the kitchen for about half an hour I decided to go into the voorhuis. It seemed a long way, now, from the kitchen to the voorhuis, and I had to lean against the wall several times to think. I passed a number of other men who were also leaning against the wall like that, thinking. One man even found that he could think best by sitting on the floor with his head in his arms.

You could see that Willem Prinsloo made good peach brandy.

Then I saw Fritz Pretorius, and the sight of him brought me to my senses right away. Airily flapping his white handkerchief in time with the music, he was talking to a girl who smiled up at him with bright eyes and red lips and small white teeth.

I knew at once that it was Grieta.

She was tall and slender and very pretty, and her dark hair was braided with a wreath of white roses that you could see had been picked that same morning in Zeerust. And she didn't look the sort of girl, either, in whose presence you had to appear clever and educated. In fact, I felt I wouldn't really need the twelve times table which I had torn off the back of a school writing book and had thrust into my jacket pocket before leaving home.

You can imagine that it was not too easy for me to get a word in with Grieta while Fritz was hanging around. But I managed it eventually, and while I was talking to her I had the satisfaction of seeing, out of the corner of my eye, the direction Fritz took. He went into the kitchen, flapping his handkerchief behind him – into the kitchen, where the laughter was, and the singing, and Willem Prinsloo's peach brandy.

I told Grieta that I was Schalk Lourens.

"Oh, yes, I have heard of you," she answered, "from Fritz Pretorius."

I knew what that meant. So I told her that Fritz was known all over the Marico for his lies. I told her other things about Fritz. Ten minutes later, when I was still talking about him, Grieta smiled and said that I could tell her the rest some other night.

"But I must tell you one more thing now," I insisted. "When he knew that he would be meeting you here at the dance, Fritz started doing homework."

I told her about the slate and the sums, and Grieta laughed softly. It struck me again how pretty she was. And her eyes were radiant in the candlelight. And the roses looked very white against her dark hair. And all this time the dancers whirled around us, and the band in the voorhuis played lively dance tunes, and from the kitchen there issued weird sounds of jubilation.

The rest happened very quickly.

I can't even remember how it all came about. But what I do know is that when we were outside, under the tall trees, with the stars over us, I could easily believe that Grieta was not a girl at all, but one of the witches of Abjaterskop who wove strange spells.

Yet to listen to my talking nobody would have guessed the wild, thrilling things that were in my heart.

I told Grieta about last year's drought, and about the difficulty of keeping the white ants from eating through the door and window-frames, and about the way my new brown boots tended to take the skin off my toe if I walked quickly.

Then I moved close up to her.

"Grieta," I said, taking her hand, "Grieta, there is something I want to tell you."

She pulled away her hand. She did it very gently, though. Sorrowfully, almost.

"I know what you want to say," she answered.

31

I was surprised at that.

"How do you know, Grieta?" I asked.

"Oh, I know lots of things," she replied, laughing again, "I haven't been to finishing school for nothing."

"I don't mean that," I answered at once, "I wasn't going to talk about spelling or arithmetic. I was going to tell you that – "

"Please don't say it, Schalk," Grieta interrupted me. "I – I don't know whether I am worthy of hearing it. I don't know, even – "

"But you are so lovely," I exclaimed. "I have got to tell you how lovely you are."

But at the very moment I stepped forward she retreated swiftly, eluding me. I couldn't understand how she had timed it so well. For, try as I might, I couldn't catch her. She sped lightly and gracefully amongst the trees, and I followed as best I could.

Yet it was not only my want of learning that handicapped me. There were also my new boots. And Willem Prinsloo's peach brandy. And the shaft of a mule-cart – the lower end of the shaft, where it rests in the grass.

I didn't fall very hard, though. The grass was long and thick there. But even as I fell a great happiness came into my heart. And I didn't care about anything else in the world.

Grieta had stopped running. She turned round. For an instant her body, slender and misty in the shadows, swayed towards me. Then her hand flew to her hair. Her finger pulled at the wreath. And the next thing I knew was that there lay, within reach of my hand, a small white rose.

I shall always remember the thrill with which I picked up that rose, and how I trembled when I stuck it in my hat. I shall always remember the stir I caused when I walked into the kitchen. Everybody stopped drinking to look at the rose in my hat. The young men made jokes about it. The older men winked slyly and patted me on the back.

Although Fritz Pretorius was not in the kitchen to witness my triumph, I knew he would get to hear of it somehow. That would make him realise that it was impudence for a fellow like him to set up as Schalk Lourens's rival.

During the rest of the night I was a hero.

The men in the kitchen made me sit on the table. They plied me with brandy and drank to my health. And afterwards, when a dozen of them carried me outside, on to an ox-wagon, for fresh air, they fell with me only once.

At daybreak I was still on that wagon.

I woke up feeling very sick – until I remembered about Grieta's rose. There was that white rose still stuck in my hat, for the whole world to know that Grieta Prinsloo had chosen me before all other men.

But what I didn't want people to know was that I had remained asleep on that ox-wagon hours after the other guests had gone. So I rode away very quietly, glad that nobody was astir to see me go.

My head was dizzy as I rode, but in my heart it felt like green wings beating; and although it was day now, there was the same soft wind in the grass that had been there when Grieta flung the rose at me, standing under the stars.

I rode slowly through the trees on the slope of Abjaterskop, and had reached the place where the path turns south again, when I saw something that made me wonder if, at these fashionable finishing schools, they did not perhaps teach the girls too much.

First I saw Fritz Pretorius's horse by the roadside.

Then I saw Fritz. He was sitting up against a thorn-tree, with his chin resting on his knees. He looked very pale and sick. But what made me wonder much about those finishing schools was that in Fritz's hat, which had fallen on the ground some distance away from him, there was a small white rose.

In the Withaak's Shade

LEOPARDS? – Oom Schalk Lourens said – Oh, yes, there are two varieties on this side of the Limpopo. The chief difference between them is that the one kind of leopard has got a few more spots on it than the other kind. But when you meet a leopard in the veld, unexpectedly, you seldom trouble to count his spots to find out what kind he belongs to. That is unnecessary. Because, whatever kind of leopard it is that you come across in this way, you only do one kind of running. And that is the fastest kind.

I remember the occasion that I came across a leopard unexpectedly, and to this day I couldn't tell you how many spots he had, even though I had all the time I needed for studying him. It happened about midday, when I was out on the far end of my farm, behind a koppie, looking for some strayed cattle. I thought the cattle might be there because it is shady under those withaak trees, and there is soft grass that is very pleasant to sit on. After I had looked for the cattle for about an hour in this manner, sitting up against a tree-trunk, it occurred to me that I could look for them just as well, or perhaps even better, if I lay down flat. For even a child knows that cattle aren't so small that you have got to get on to stilts and things to see them properly.

So I lay on my back, with my hat tilted over my face, and my legs crossed, and when I closed my eyes slightly the tip of my boot, sticking up into the air, looked just like the peak of Abjaterskop.

Overhead a lone aasvoël wheeled, circling slowly round and round without flapping his wings, and I knew that not even a calf could pass in any part of the sky between the tip of my toe and that aasvoël without my observing it immediately. What was more, I could go on lying there under the withaak and looking for the cattle like that all day, if necessary. As you know, I am not the sort of farmer to loaf about the house when there is man's work to be done.

The more I screwed up my eyes and gazed at the toe of my boot, the more it looked like Abjaterskop. By and by it seemed that it actually was Abjaterskop, and I could see the stones on top of it, and the bush trying to grow up its sides, and in my ears there was a far-off, humming sound, like bees in an orchard on a still day. As I have said, it was very pleasant.

Then a strange thing happened. It was as though a huge cloud, shaped like an animal's head and with spots on it, had settled on top of Abjaterskop. It seemed so funny that I wanted to laugh. But I didn't. Instead, I opened my eyes a little more and felt glad to think that I was only dreaming. Because otherwise I would have to believe that the spotted cloud on Abjaterskop was actually a leopard, and that he was gazing at my boot. Again I wanted to laugh. But then, suddenly, I knew.

And I didn't feel so glad. For it was a leopard, all right – a large-sized, hungry-looking leopard, and he was sniffing suspiciously at my feet. I was uncomfortable. I knew that nothing I could do would ever convince that leopard that my toe was Abjaterskop. He was not that sort of leopard: I knew that without even counting the number of his spots. Instead, having finished with my feet, he started sniffing higher up. It was the most terrifying moment of my life. I wanted to get up and run for it. But I couldn't. My legs wouldn't work.

Every big-game hunter I have come across has told me the same story about how, at one time or another, he has owed his escape from lions and other wild animals to his cunning in lying down and pre-tending to be dead, so that the beast of prey loses interest in him and walks off. Now, as I lay there on the grass, with the leopard trying to make up his mind about me, I understood why, in such a situation, the hunter doesn't move. It's simply that he can't move. That's all. It's not his cunning that keeps him down. It's his legs.

In the meantime, the leopard had got up as far as my knees. He was studying my trousers very carefully, and I started getting embarrassed. My trousers were old and rather unfashionable. Also, at the knee, there was a torn place, from where I had climbed through a barbed-wire fence, into the thick bush, the time I saw the Government tax-collector coming over the bult before he saw me. The leopard stared at that rent in my trousers for quite a while, and my embarrassment grew. I felt I wanted to explain about the Government tax-collector and the barbed wire. I didn't want the leopard to get the impression that Schalk Lourens was the sort of man who didn't care about his personal appear-ance.

When the leopard got as far as my shirt, however, I felt better. It was a good blue flannel shirt that I had bought only a few weeks ago from the Indian store at Ramoutsa, and I didn't care how many strange leop-ards saw it. Nevertheless, I made up my mind that next time I went to

35

lie on the grass under the withaak, looking for strayed cattle, I would first polish up my veldskoens with sheep's fat, and I would put on my black hat that I only wear to Nagmaal. I could not permit the wild animals of the neighbourhood to sneer at me.

But when the leopard reached my face I got frightened again. I knew he couldn't take exception to my shirt. But I wasn't so sure about my face. Those were terrible moments. I lay very still, afraid to open my eyes and afraid to breathe. Sniff-sniff, the huge creature went, and his breath swept over my face in hot gasps. You hear of many frightening experiences that a man has in a lifetime. I have also been in quite a few perilous situations. But if you want something to make you suddenly old and to turn your hair white in a few moments, there is nothing to beat a leopard – especially when he is standing over you, with his jaws at your throat, trying to find a good place to bite.

The leopard gave a deep growl, stepped right over my body, knocking off my hat, and growled again. I opened my eyes and saw the animal moving away clumsily. But my relief didn't last long. The leopard didn't move far. Instead, he turned over and lay down next to me.

Yes, there on the grass, in the shade of the withaak, the leopard and I lay down together. The leopard lay half-curled up, on his side, with his forelegs crossed, like a dog, and whenever I tried to move away he grunted. I am sure that in the whole history of the Groot Marico there have never been two stranger companions engaged in the thankless task of looking for strayed cattle.

Next day, in Fanie Snyman's voorkamer, which was used as a post office, I told my story to the farmers of the neighbourhood, while they were drinking coffee and waiting for the motor-lorry from Zeerust.

"And how did you get away from that leopard in the end?" Koos van Tonder asked, trying to be funny. "I suppose you crawled through the grass and frightened the leopard off by pretending to be a python."

"No, I just got up and walked home," I said. "I remembered that the cattle I was looking for might have gone the other way and strayed into your kraal. I thought they would be safer with the leopard."

"Did the leopard tell you what he thought of General Pienaar's last speech in the Volksraad?" Frans Welman asked, and they all laughed.

I told my story over several times before the lorry came with our letters, and although the dozen odd men present didn't say much while I was talking, I could see that they listened to me in the same way that they listened when Krisjan Lemmer talked. And everybody knew that Krisjan Lemmer was the biggest liar in the Bushveld.

To make matters worse, Krisjan Lemmer was there, too, and when I got to the part of my story where the leopard lay down beside me, Krisjan Lemmer winked at me. You know that kind of wink. It was to let me know that there was now a new understanding between us, and that we could speak in future as one Marico liar to another.

I didn't like that.

"Kêrels," I said in the end, "I know just what you are thinking. You don't believe me, and you don't want to say so."

"But we do believe you," Krisjan Lemmer interrupted me, "very wonderful things happen in the Bushveld. I once had a twenty-foot mamba that I named Hans. This snake was so attached to me that I couldn't go anywhere without him. He would even follow me to church on a Sunday, and because he didn't care much for some of the sermons, he would wait for me outside under a tree. Not that Hans was irreligious. But he had a sensitive nature, and the strong line that the predikant took against the serpent in the Garden of Eden always made Hans feel awkward. Yet he didn't go and look for a withaak to lie under, like your leopard. He wasn't stand-offish in that way. An ordinary thorn-tree's shade was good enough for Hans. He knew he was only a mamba, and didn't try to give himself airs."

I didn't take any notice of Krisjan Lemmer's stupid lies, but the upshot of this whole affair was that I also began to have doubts about the existence of that leopard. I recalled queer stories I had heard of human beings that could turn themselves into animals, and although I am not a superstitious man I could not shake off the feeling that it was a spook thing that had happened. But when, a few days later, a huge leopard had been seen from the roadside near the poort, and then again by Mtosas on the way to Nietverdiend, and again in the turf-lands near the Malopo, matters took a different turn.

At first people jested about this leopard. They said it wasn't a real leopard, but a spotted animal that had walked away out of Schalk Lourens's dream. They also said that the leopard had come to the Dwarsberge to have a look at Krisjan Lemmer's twenty-foot mamba. But afterwards, when they had found his spoor at several waterholes, they had no more doubt about the leopard.

It was dangerous to walk about in the veld, they said. Exciting times followed. There was a great deal of shooting at the leopard and a great deal of running away from him. The amount of Martini and Mauser fire I heard in the krantzes reminded me of nothing so much as the First Boer War. And the amount of running away reminded me of nothing so much as the Second Boer War.

But always the leopard escaped unharmed. Somehow, I felt sorry for him. The way he had first sniffed at me and then lain down beside me that day under the withaak was a strange thing that I couldn't understand. I thought of the Bible, where it is written that the lion shall lie down with the lamb.

But I also wondered if I hadn't dreamt it all. The manner in which those things had befallen me was all so unearthly. The leopard began to take up a lot of my thoughts. And there was no man to whom I could talk about it who would be able to help me in any way. Even now, as I am telling you this story, I am expecting you to wink at me, like Krisjan Lemmer did.

Still, I can only tell you the things that happened as I saw them, and what the rest was about only Africa knows.

It was some time before I again walked along the path that leads through the bush to where the withaaks are. But I didn't lie down on the grass again. Because when I reached the place, I found that the leopard had got there before me. He was lying on the same spot, half-curled up in the withaak's shade, and his forepaws were folded as a dog's are, sometimes. But he lay very still. And even from the distance where I stood I could see the red splash on his breast where a Mauser bullet had gone.

Ox-wagons on Trek

WHEN I see the rain beating white on the thorn-trees, as it does now (Oom Schalk Lourens said), I remember another time when it rained. And there was a girl in an ox-wagon who dreamed. And in answer to her dreaming a lover came, galloping to her side from out of the veld. But he tarried only a short while, this lover who had come to her from the mist of the rain and the warmth of her dreams.

And yet when he had gone there was a slow look in her eyes that must have puzzled her lover very much, for it was a look of satisfaction, almost.

There had been rain all the way up from Sephton's Nek, that time. And the five ox-wagons on the road to the north rolled heavily through the mud. We had been to Zeerust for the Nagmaal church service, which we attended once a year.

You know what it is with these Nagmaals.

The Lord spreads these festivities over so many days that you have not only got time to go to church, but you also get a chance of going to the bioscope. Sometimes you even get a chance of going to the bar. But then you must go in the back way, through the dark passage next to the draper's shop.

Because Zeerust is a small place, and if you are seen going into the bar during Nagmaal people are liable to talk. I can still remember how surprised I was one morning when I went into that dark passage next to the draper's shop and found the predikant there, wiping his mouth. The predikant looked at me and shook his head solemnly, and I felt very guilty.

So I went to the bioscope instead.

The house was very crowded. I couldn't follow much of the picture at the beginning, but afterwards a little boy who sat next to me and understood English explained to me what it was all about.

There was a young man who had the job of what he called taking people for a ride. Afterwards he got into trouble with the police. But he was a good-looking young man, and his sweetheart was very sorry for him when they took him into a small room and fastened him down on to a sort of chair.

I can't tell what they did that for. All I know is that I have been a
Boer War prisoner at St. Helena, and they never gave me a chair to sit
on. Only a long wooden bench that I had to scrub once a week.

Anyway, I don't know what happened to the young man after that,
because he was still sitting in that chair when the band started playing
an English hymn about King George, and everybody stood up.

And a few days later five ox-wagons, full of people who had been to
the Zeerust Nagmaal, were trekking along the road that led back to the
Groot Marico. Inside the wagon-tents sat the women and children, listening to the rain pelting against the canvas. By the side of the oxen the
drivers walked, cracking their long whips while the rain beat in their
faces.

Overhead everything was black, except for the frequent flashes of
lightning that tore across the sky.

After I had walked in this manner for some time, I began to get
lonely. So I handed my whip to the kaffir voorloper and went on ahead
to Adriaan Brand's wagon. For some distance I walked in silence
beside Adriaan, who had his trousers rolled up to his knees, and had
much trouble to brandish his whip and at the same time keep the rain
out of his pipe.

"It's Minnie," Adriaan Brand said suddenly, referring to his nine-
teen-year-old daughter. "There is one place in Zeerust that Minnie
should not go to. And every Nagmaal, to my sorrow, I find she has
been there. And it all goes to her head."

"Oh, yes," I answered. "It always does."

All the same, I was somewhat startled at Adriaan's remarks. Minnie
didn't strike me as the sort of girl who would go and spend her father's
money drinking peach brandy in the bar. I started wondering if she had
seen me in that draper's passage. Then Adriaan went on talking and I
felt more at ease.

"The place where they show those moving pictures," he explained.
"Every time Minnie goes there, she comes back with ideas that are useless for a farmer's daughter. But this last time has made her quite
impossible. For one thing, she says she won't marry Frans du Toit anymore. She says Frans is too honest."

"Well, that needn't be a difficulty, Adriaan," I said. "You can teach
Frans du Toit a few of the things you have done. That will make him
dishonest enough. Like the way you put your brand on those oxen that

strayed into your kraal. Or the way you altered the figures on the compensation forms after the rinderpest. Or the way – "

Adriaan looked at me with some disfavour.

"It isn't that," he interrupted me, while I was still trying to call to mind a lot of other things that he was able to teach Frans du Toit, "Minnie wants a mysterious sort of man. She wants a man who is dishonest, but who has got foreign manners and a good heart. She saw a man like that at the picture place she went to, and since then – "

We both looked round together.

Through the mist of the white rain a horseman came galloping up towards our wagons. He rode fast. Adriaan Brand and I stood and watched him.

By this time our wagons were some distance behind the others.

The horseman came thundering along at full gallop until he was abreast of us. Then he pulled up sharply, jerking the horse on to his hind legs.

The stranger told us that his name was Koos Fichardt and that he was on his way to the Bechuanaland Protectorate. Adriaan Brand and I introduced ourselves, and shortly afterwards Fichardt accepted our invitation to spend the night with us.

We outspanned a mile or so farther on, drawing the five wagons up close together and getting what shelter we could by spreading bucksails.

Next morning there was no more rain. By that time Koos Fichardt had seen Adriaan Brand's daughter Minnie. So he decided to stay with us longer.

We trekked on again, and from where I walked beside my oxen I could see Koos Fichardt and Minnie. They sat at the back of Adriaan Brand's wagon, hatless, with their legs hanging down and the morning breeze blowing through their hair, and it was evident that Minnie was fascinated by the stranger. Also, he seemed to be very much interested in her.

You do get like that, when there is suddenly a bright morning after long rains, and a low wind stirs the wet grass, and you feel, for a little while, that you know the same things that the veld knows, and in your heart are whisperings.

Most of the time they sat holding hands, Fichardt talking a great deal and Minnie nodding her pretty head at intervals and encouraging him to continue. And they were all lies he told her, I suppose, as only a young man in love really can tell lies.

I remembered what Adriaan had told me about the ideas Minnie had got after she had been to the bioscope. And when I looked carefully at Fichardt I perceived that in many respects he was like that man I saw in the picture who was being fastened on to a chair.

Fichardt was tall and dark and well dressed. He walked with a swagger. He had easy and engaging manners, and we all liked him.

But I noticed one or two peculiar things about Koos Fichardt. For instance, shortly after our wagons had entered a clump of tall camel-thorn trees, we heard horses galloping towards us. It turned out that the riders were a couple of farmers living in the neighbourhood. But as soon as he heard the hoof-beats, Koos Fichardt let go of Minnie's hand and crept under a bucksail.

It would be more correct to say that he dived under – he was so quick.

I said to myself that Fichardt's action might have no meaning, of course. After all, it is quite permissible for a man to feel that he would suddenly like to take a look at what is underneath the bucksail he is sitting on. Also, if he wants to, there is no harm in his spending quite a while on this task. And it is only natural, after he has had a bucksail on top of him, that he should come out with his hair rather ruffled, and that his face should be pale.

That night, when we outspanned next to the Groen River, it was very pleasant. We all gathered round the camp-fire and roasted meat and cooked crushed mealies. We sang songs and told ghost stories. And I wondered what Frans du Toit – the honest youth whom Minnie had discarded in Zeerust – would have thought if he could see Minnie Brand and Koos Fichardt, sitting unashamedly in each other's arms, for all the world to see their love, while the light of the camp-fire cast a rich glow over the thrill that was on their faces.

And although I knew how wonderful were the passing moments for those two, yet somehow, somehow, because I had seen so much of the world, I also felt sorry for them.

The next day we did not trek.

The Groen River was in flood from the heavy rains, and Oupa van Tonder, who had lived a long time in the Cape and was well versed in the ways of rivers, and knew how to swim, even, told us that it would not be safe to cross the drift for another twenty-four hours. Accordingly, we decided to remain camped out where we were until next morning.

At first Koos Fichardt was much disturbed by this news, explaining how necessary it was for him to get into the Bechuanaland Protectorate by a certain day. After a while, however, he seemed to grow more reconciled to the necessity of waiting until the river had gone down.

But I noticed that he frequently gazed out over the veld in the direction from which we had come. He gazed out rather anxiously, I thought.

Some of the men went shooting. Others remained at their wagons, doing odd jobs to the yokes or the trek-chains. Koos Fichardt made himself useful in various little ways, amongst other things, helping Minnie with the cooking. They laughed and romped a good deal.

Night came, and the occupants of the five wagons again gathered round the blazing fire. In some ways, that night was even grander than the one before. The songs we sang were more rousing. The stories we told seemed to have more power in them.

There was much excitement the following morning by the time the wagons were ready to go through the drift. And the excitement did not lie only in the bustle of inspanning the oxen.

For when we crossed the river it was without Koos Fichardt, and there was a slow look in Minnie's eyes.

The wagons creaked and splashed into the water, and we saw Koos Fichardt for the last time, sitting on his horse, with a horseman in uniform on each side of him. And when he took off his hat in farewell he had to use both hands, because of the cuffs that held his wrists together.

But always what I will remember is that slow look in Minnie's eyes. It was a kind of satisfaction, almost, at the thought that all the things that came to the girl she saw in the picture had now come to her, too.

The Music Maker

O F course, I know about history – Oom Schalk Lourens said – it's the stuff children learn in school. Only the other day, at Thys Lemmer's post office, Thys's little son Stoffel started reading out of his history book about a man called Vasco da Gama, who visited the Cape. At once Dirk Snyman started telling young Stoffel about the time when he himself visited the Cape, but young Stoffel didn't take much notice of him. So Dirk Snyman said that that showed you.

Anyway, Dirk Snyman said that what he wanted to tell young Stoffel was that the last time he went down to the Cape a kaffir came and sat down right next to him in a tram. What was more, Dirk Snyman said, was that people seemed to think nothing of it.

Yes, it's a queer thing about wanting to get into history.

Take the case of Manie Kruger, for instance.

Manie Kruger was one of the best farmers in the Marico. He knew just how much peach brandy to pour out for the tax-collector to make sure that he would nod dreamily at everything Manie said. And at a time of drought Manie Kruger could run to the Government for help much quicker than any man I ever knew.

Then one day Manie Kruger read an article in the *Kerkbode* about a musician who said that he knew more about music than Napoleon did. After that – having first read another article to find out who Napoleon was – Manie Kruger was a changed man. He could talk of nothing but his place in history and of his musical career.

Of course, everybody knew that no man in the Marico could be counted in the same class with Manie Kruger when it came to playing the concertina.

No Bushveld dance was complete without Manie Kruger's concertina. When he played a vastrap you couldn't keep your feet still. But after he had decided to become the sort of musician that gets into history books, it was strange the way that Manie Kruger altered. For one thing, he said he would never again play at a dance. We all felt sad about that. It was not easy to think of the Bushveld dances of the future. There would be the peach brandy in the kitchen; in the voorkamer the feet of the dancers would go through the steps of the schottische and the polka and the waltz and the mazurka, but on the riempies bench in the corner, where the musicians sat, there would be no Manie Kruger. And they would play "Die Vaal Hare en die Blou Oge" and "Vat Jou Goed en Trek, Ferreira," but it would be another's fingers that swept over the concertina keys. And when, with the dancing and the peach brandy, the young men called out "Dagbreek toe!" it would not be Manie Kruger's head that bowed down to the applause.

It was sad to think about all this.

For so long, at the Bushveld dances, Manie Kruger had been the chief musician.

And of all those who mourned this change that had come over Manie, we could see that there was no one more grieved than Letta Steyn.

And Manie said such queer things at times. Once he said that what he had to do to get into history was to die of consumption in the arms of a princess, like another musician he had read about. Only it was hard to get consumption in the Marico, because the climate was so healthy.

Although Manie stopped playing his concertina at dances, he played a great deal in another way. He started giving what he called recitals. I went to several of them. They were very impressive.

At the first recital I went to, I found that the front part of Manie's voorkamer was taken up by rows of benches and chairs that he had borrowed from those of his neighbours who didn't mind having to eat their meals on candle-boxes and upturned buckets. At the far end of the voorkamer a wide green curtain was hung on a piece of string. When I came in the place was full. I managed to squeeze in on a bench between Jan Terreblanche and a young woman in a blue kappie. Jan Terreblanche had been trying to hold this young woman's hand.

Manie Kruger was sitting behind the green curtain. He was already there when I came in. I knew it was Manie by his veldskoens, which were sticking out from underneath the curtain. Letta Steyn sat in front of me. Now and again, when she turned round, I saw that there was a flush on her face and a look of dark excitement in her eyes.

At last everything was ready, and Joel, the farm kaffir to whom Manie had given this job, slowly drew the green curtain aside. A few of the younger men called out "Middag, ou Manie," and Jan Terreblanche asked if it wasn't very close and suffocating, sitting there like that behind that piece of green curtain.

Then he started to play.

And we all knew that it was the most wonderful concertina music we had ever listened to. It was Manie Kruger at his best. He had practised a long time for that recital; his fingers flew over the keys; the notes of the concertina swept into our hearts; the music of Manie Kruger lifted us right out of that voorkamer into a strange and rich and dazzling world.

It was fine.

The applause right through was terrific. At the end of each piece the kaffir closed the curtains in front of Manie, and we sat waiting for a few minutes until the curtains were drawn aside again. But after that first time there was no more laughter about this procedure. The recital lasted for about an hour and a half, and the applause at the end was even greater than at the start. And during those ninety minutes Manie left his seat only once. That was when there was some trouble with the curtain and he got up to kick the kaffir.

At the end of the recital Manie did not come forward and shake hands with us, as we had expected. Instead, he slipped through behind the green curtain into the kitchen, and sent word that we could come and see him round the back. At first we thought this a bit queer, but Letta Steyn said it was all right. She explained that in other countries the great musicians and stage performers all received their admirers at the back. Jan Terreblanche said that if these actors used their kitchens for entertaining their visitors in, he wondered where they did their cooking.

Nevertheless, most of us went round to the kitchen, and we had a good time congratulating Manie Kruger and shaking hands with him; and Manie spoke much of his musical future, and of the triumphs that would come to him in the great cities of the world, when he would stand before the curtain and bow to the applause.

Manie gave a number of other recitals after that. They were all equally fine. Only, as he had to practise all day, he couldn't pay much attention to his farming. The result was that his farm went to pieces and he got into debt. The court messengers came and attached half his cattle while he was busy practising for his fourth recital. And he was practising for his seventh recital when they took away his ox-wagon and mule-cart.

Eventually, when Manie Kruger's musical career reached that stage when they took away his plough and the last of his oxen, he sold up what remained of his possessions and left the Bushveld, on his way to those great cities that he had so often talked about. It was very grand, the send-off that the Marico gave him. The predikant and the Volksraad member both made speeches about how proud the Transvaal was of her great son. Then Manie replied. Instead of thanking his audience, however, he started abusing us left and right, calling us a mob of hooligans and soulless Philistines, and saying how much he despised us.

Naturally, we were very much surprised at this outburst, as we had always been kind to Manie Kruger and had encouraged him all we could. But Letta Steyn explained that Manie didn't really mean the things he said. She said it was just that every great artist was expected to talk in that way about the place he came from.

So we knew it was all right, and the more offensive the things were that Manie said about us, the louder we shouted "Hoor, hoor vir Manie." There was a particularly enthusiastic round of applause when he said that we knew as much about art as a boomslang. His language was hotter than anything I had ever heard – except once. And that was when De Wet said what he thought of Cronje's surrender to the English at Paardeberg. We could feel that Manie's speech was the real thing. We cheered ourselves hoarse, that day.

And so Manie Kruger went. We received one letter to say that he had reached Pretoria. But after that we heard no more from him.

Yet always, when Letta Steyn spoke of Manie, it was as a child speaks of a dream, half wistfully, and always, with the voice of a wistful child, she would tell me how one day, one day he would return. And often, when it was dusk, I would see her sitting on the stoep, gazing out across the veld into the evening, down the dusty road that led between the thorn-trees and beyond the Dwarsberg, waiting for the lover who would come to her no more.

It was a long time before I again saw Manie Kruger. And then it was in Pretoria. I had gone there to interview the Volksraad member about an election promise. It was quite by accident that I saw Manie. And he was playing the concertina – playing as well as ever, I thought. I went away quickly. But what affected me very strangely was just that one glimpse I had of the green curtain of the bar in front of which Manie Kruger played.

Marico Scandal

WHEN I passed young Gawie Erasmus by the wall of the new dam (Oom Schalk Lourens said) I could see clearly that he had had another disagreement with his employer, Koos Deventer. Because, as Gawie walked away from me, I saw, on the seat of his trousers, the still damp imprint of a muddy boot. The dried mud of another footprint, higher up on his trousers, told of a similar disagreement that Gawie had had with his employer on the previous day. I thought that Gawie must be a high-spirited young man to disagree so frequently with his employer.

Nevertheless, I felt it my duty to speak to Koos Deventer about this matter when I sat with him in his voorkamer, drinking coffee.

"I see that Gawie Erasmus still lays the stones unevenly on the wall of the new dam you are building," I said to Koos Deventer.

"Indeed," Koos answered, "have you been looking at the front part of the wall?"

"No," I said, "I have been looking at Gawie's trousers. The back part of the trousers."

"The trouble with Gawie Erasmus," Koos said, "is that he is not really a white man. It doesn't show in his hair or his fingernails, of course. He is not as coloured as all that. But you can tell it easily in other ways. Yes, that is what's wrong with Gawie. His Hottentot forebears."

At that moment Koos Deventer's eldest daughter, Francina, brought us in more coffee.

"It is not true, father, what you said about Gawie Erasmus," Francina said. "Gawie is white. He is as white as I am."

Francina was eighteen. She was tall and slender. She had a neat figure. And she looked very pretty in that voorkamer, with the yellow hair falling on to her cheeks from underneath a blue ribbon. Another thing I noticed about Francina, as she moved daintily towards me with the tray, was the scent that she bought in Zeerust at the last Nagmaal. The perfume lay on her strangely, like the night.

Koos Deventer made no reply to Francina. And only after she had gone back into the kitchen, and the door was closed, did he return to the subject of Gawie Erasmus.

"He is so coloured," Koos said, "that he even sleeps with a blanket over his head, like a kaffir does."

It struck me that Koos Deventer's statements were rather peculiar. For, according to Koos, you couldn't tell that Gawie Erasmus was coloured, just by looking at his hair and fingernails. You had to wait until Gawie lay underneath a blanket, so that you saw nothing of him at all.

But I remembered the way that Francina had walked out of the voorkamer with her head very high and her red lips closed. And it seemed to me, then, that Gawie's disagreements with his employer were not all due to the unevenness of the wall of the new dam. I did not see Gawie Erasmus again until the meeting of the Drogevlei Debating Society.

But in the meantime the story that Gawie was coloured gained much ground. Paulus Welman said that he knew a man once in Vryburg who had known Gawie's grandfather. And this man said that Gawie's grandfather had a big belly and wore a copper ring through his nose. At other times, again, Paulus Welman said that it was Gawie's father whom this man in Vryburg had known, and that Gawie's father did not wear the copper ring in his nose, but in his one ear. It was hard to know which story to believe. So most of the farmers in the Marico believed both.

The meeting of the Drogevlei Debating Society was held in the schoolroom. There was a good attendance. For the debate was to be on the Native Question. And that was always a popular subject in the Marico. You could say much about it without having to think hard.

I was standing under the thorn-trees talking to Paulus Welman and some others, when Koos Deventer arrived with his wife and Francina and Gawie. They got off the mule-cart, and the two women walked on towards the schoolroom. Koos and Gawie stayed behind, hitching the reins on to a tree. Several of the men with me shook their heads gravely at what they saw. For Gawie, while stooping for a riem, had another hurried disagreement with his employer.

Francina, walking with her mother towards the school, sensed that something was amiss. But when she turned round she was too late to see anything.

Francina and her mother greeted us as they passed. Paulus Welman said that Francina was a pretty girl, but rather stand-offish. He said her understanding was a bit slow, too. He said that when he had told her that joke about the copper ring in the one ear of Gawie's father, Francina looked at him as though he had said there was a copper ring in his own ear. She didn't seem to be quite all there, Paulus Welman said.

But I didn't take much notice of Paulus.

I stood there, under the thorn-tree, where Francina had passed, and I breathed in stray breaths of that scent which Francina had bought in Zeerust. It was a sweet and strange fragrance. But it was sad, also, like youth that has gone.

I waited in the shadows. Gawie Erasmus came by. I scrutinised him carefully, but except that his hair was black and his skin rather dark, there seemed to be no justification for Koos Deventer to say that he was coloured. It looked like some kind of joke that Koos Deventer and Paulus Welman had got up between them. Gawie seemed to be just an ordinary and rather good-looking youth of about twenty.

By this time it was dark. Oupa van Tonder, an old farmer who was very keen on debates, lit an oil-lamp that he had brought with him and put it on the table.

The schoolmaster took the chair, as usual. He said that, as we all knew, the subject was that the Bantu should be allowed to develop along his own lines. He said he had got the idea for this debate from an article he had read in the *Kerkbode*.

Oupa van Tonder then got up and said that, the way the schoolmaster put it, the subject was too hard to understand. He proposed, for the sake of the older debaters, who had not gone to school much, that they should just be allowed to talk about how the kaffirs in the Marico were getting cheekier every day. The older debaters cheered Oupa van Tonder for putting the schoolmaster in his place.

Oupa van Tonder was still talking when the schoolmaster banged the table with a ruler and said that he was out of order. Oupa van Tonder got really annoyed then. He said he had lived in the Transvaal for eighty-eight years, and this was the first time in his life that he had been so insulted. "Anybody would think that I am the steam machine that threshes the mealies at Nietverdiend, that I can get out of order," Oupa van Tonder said.

Some of the men started pulling Oupa van Tonder by his jacket to get him to sit down, but others shouted out that he was quite right, and that they should pull the schoolmaster's jacket instead.

The schoolmaster explained that if some people were talking on the *Kerkbode* subject, and others were talking on Oupa van Tonder's subject, it would mean that there were two different debates going on at the same time. Oupa van Tonder said that that was quite all right. It suited him, he said. And he told a long story about a kaffir who had stolen his trek-chain. He also said that if the schoolmaster kept on banging the table like that, while he was talking, he would go home and take his oil-lamp with him.

In the end the schoolmaster said that we could talk about anything we liked. Only, he asked us not to use any of that coarse language that had spoilt the last three debates. "Try to remember that there are ladies present," he said in a weak sort of way.

The older debaters, who had not been to school much, spoke at great length.

Afterwards the schoolmaster suggested that perhaps some of our younger members would like to debate a little, and he called on Gawie Erasmus to say a few words on behalf of the kaffirs. The schoolmaster spoke playfully.

Koos Deventer guffawed behind his hand. Some of the women tittered. On account of his unpopularity the schoolmaster heard little of what went on in the Marico. The only news he got was what he could glean from reading the compositions of the children in the higher classes. And we could see that the children had not yet mentioned, in their compositions, that Gawie Erasmus was supposed to be coloured.

You know how it is with a scandalous story. The last one to hear it is always that person that the scandal is about.

That crowd in the schoolroom realised quickly what the situation was. And there was much laughter all the time that Gawie spoke. I can still remember that half-perplexed look on his dark face, as though he had meant to make a funny speech, but had not expected quite that amount of appreciation. And I noticed that Francina's face was very red, and that her eyes were fixed steadily on the floor.

There was so much laughter, finally, that Gawie had to sit down, still looking slightly puzzled.

After that Paulus Welman got up and told funny stories about so-called white people whose grandfathers had big bellies and wore copper rings in their ears. I don't know at what stage of the debate Gawie

Erasmus found out at whom these funny remarks were being directed. Or when it was that he slipped out of the schoolroom, to leave Drogevlei and the Groot Marico for ever.

And some months later, when I again went to visit Koos Deventer, he did not once mention Gawie Erasmus to me. He seemed to have grown tired of Marico scandals. But when Francina brought in the coffee, it was as though she thought that Koos had again spoken about Gawie. For she looked at him in a disapproving sort of way and said: "Gawie is white, father. He is as white as I am."

I could not at first make out what the change was that had come over Francina. She was as good-looking as ever, but in a different sort of way. I began to think that perhaps it was because she no longer wore that strange perfume that she bought in Zeerust.

But at that moment she brought me my coffee.

And I saw then, when she came towards me from behind the table, with the tray, why it was that Francina Deventer moved so heavily.

Mafeking Road

W HEN people ask me – as they often do – how it is that I can tell the best stories of anybody in the Transvaal (Oom Schalk Lourens said, modestly), then I explain to them that I just learn through observing the way that the world has with men and women. When I say this they nod their heads wisely, and say that they understand, and I nod my head wisely also, and that seems to satisfy them. But the thing I say to them is a lie, of course.

For it is not the story that counts. What matters is the way you tell it. The important thing is to know just at what moment you must knock out your pipe on your veldskoen, and at what stage of the story you must start talking about the School Committee at Drogevlei. Another necessary thing is to know what part of the story to leave out.

And you can never learn these things.

Look at Floris, the last of the Van Barnevelts. There is no doubt that he had a good story, and he should have been able to get people to listen to it. And yet nobody took any notice of him or of the things he had to say. Just because he couldn't tell the story properly.

Accordingly, it made me sad whenever I listened to him talk. For I could tell just where he went wrong. He never knew the moment at which to knock the ash out of his pipe. He always mentioned his opinion of the Drogevlei School Committee in the wrong place. And, what was still worse, he didn't know what part of the story to leave out.

And it was no use my trying to teach him, because as I have said, this is the thing that you can never learn. And so, each time he had told his story, I would see him turn away from me, with a look of doom on his face, and walk slowly down the road, stoop-shouldered, the last of the Van Barnevelts.

On the wall of Floris's voorkamer is a long family tree of the Van Barnevelts. You can see it there for yourself. It goes back for over two hundred years, to the Van Barnevelts of Amsterdam. At one time it went even further back, but that was before the white ants started on the top part of it and ate away quite a lot of Van Barnevelts. Nevertheless, if you look at this list, you will notice that at the bottom, under Floris's own name, there is the last entry, "Stephanus." And behind the name, "Stephanus," between two bent strokes, you will read the words: "Obiit Mafeking."

At the outbreak of the Second Boer War Floris van Barnevelt was a widower, with one son, Stephanus, who was aged seventeen. The commando from our part of the Transvaal set off very cheerfully. We made a fine show, with our horses and our wide hats and our bandoliers, and with the sun shining on the barrels of our Mausers.

Young Stephanus van Barnevelt was the gayest of us all. But he said there was one thing he didn't like about the war, and that was that, in the end, we would have to go over the sea. He said that, after we had invaded the whole of the Cape, our commando would have to go on a ship and invade England also.

But we didn't go overseas, just then. Instead, our veldkornet told us that the burghers from our part had been ordered to join the big commando that was lying at Mafeking. We had to go and shoot a man there called Baden-Powell.

We rode steadily on into the west. After a while we noticed that our veldkornet frequently got off his horse and engaged in conversation with passing kaffirs, leading them some distance from the roadside and speaking earnestly to them. Of course, it was right that our veldkornet should explain to the kaffirs that it was war-time, now, and that the Republic expected every kaffir to stop smoking so much dagga and to think seriously about what was going on. But we noticed that each time at the end of the conversation the kaffir would point towards something, and that our veldkornet would take much pains to follow the direction of the kaffir's finger.

Of course, we understood, then, what it was all about. Our veldkornet was a young fellow, and he was shy to let us see that he didn't know the way to Mafeking.

Somehow, after that, we did not have so much confidence in our veldkornet.

After a few days we got to Mafeking. We stayed there a long while, until the English troops came up and relieved the place. We left, then. We left quickly. The English troops had brought a lot of artillery with them. And if we had difficulty in finding the road to Mafeking, we had no difficulty in finding the road away from Mafeking. And this time our veldkornet did not need kaffirs, either, to point with their fingers where we had to go. Even though we did a lot of travelling in the night.

Long afterwards I spoke to an Englishman about this. He said it gave him a queer feeling to hear about the other side of the story of Mafeking. He said there had been very great rejoicings in England when Mafeking was relieved, and it was strange to think of the other aspect of it – of a defeated country and of broken columns blundering through the dark.

I remember many things that happened on the way back from Mafeking. There was no moon. And the stars shone down fitfully on the road that was full of guns and frightened horses and desperate men. The veld throbbed with the hoof-beats of baffled commandos. The stars looked down on scenes that told sombrely of a nation's ruin; they looked on the muzzles of the Mausers that had failed the Transvaal for the first time.

Of course, as a burgher of the Republic, I knew what my duty was. And that was to get as far away as I could from the place where, in the sunset, I had last seen English artillery. The other burghers knew their duty also. Our kommandants and veldkornets had to give very few orders. Nevertheless, although I rode very fast, there was one young man who rode still faster. He kept ahead of me all the time. He rode, as a burgher should ride when there may be stray bullets flying, with his head well down and with his arms almost round the horse's neck.

He was Stephanus, the young son of Floris van Barnevelt.

There was much grumbling and dissatisfaction, some time afterwards, when our leaders started making an effort to get the commandos in order again. In the end they managed to get us to halt. But most of us felt that this was a foolish thing to do. Especially as there was still a lot of firing going on, all over the place, in haphazard fashion, and we couldn't tell how far the English had followed us in the dark. Furthermore, the commandos had scattered in so many different directions that it seemed hopeless to try and get them together again until after the war. Stephanus and I dismounted and stood by our horses. Soon there was a large body of men around us. Their figures looked strange and shadowy in the starlight. Some of them stood by their horses. Others sat on the grass by the roadside. "Vas staan, burghers, vas staan," came the commands of our officers. And all the time we could still hear what sounded a lot like lyddite. It seemed foolish to be waiting there.

"The next they'll want," Stephanus van Barnevelt said, "is for us to go back to Mafeking. Perhaps our kommandant has left his tobacco pouch behind, there."

Some of us laughed at this remark, but Floris, who had not dismounted, said that Stephanus ought to be ashamed of himself for talking like that. From what we could see of Floris in the gloom, he looked quite impressive, sitting very straight in the saddle, with the stars shining on his beard and rifle.

"If the veldkornet told me to go back to Mafeking," Floris said, "I would go back."

"That's how a burgher should talk," the veldkornet said, feeling flattered. For he had had little authority since the time we found out what he was talking to the kaffirs for.

"I wouldn't go back to Mafeking for anybody," Stephanus replied, "unless, maybe, it's to hand myself over to the English."

"We can shoot you for doing that," the veldkornet said. "It's contrary to military law."

"I wish I knew something about military law," Stephanus answered. "Then I would draw up a peace treaty between Stephanus van Barnevelt and England."

Some of the men laughed again. But Floris shook his head sadly. He said the Van Barnevelts had fought bravely against Spain in a war that lasted eighty years.

Suddenly, out of the darkness there came a sharp rattle of musketry, and our men started getting uneasy again. But the sound of the firing decided Stephanus. He jumped on his horse quickly.

"I am turning back," he said, "I am going to hands-up to the English."

"No, don't go," the veldkornet called to him lamely, "or at least, wait until the morning. They may shoot you in the dark by mistake." As I have said, the veldkornet had very little authority.

Two days passed before we again saw Floris van Barnevelt. He was in a very worn and troubled state, and he said that it had been very hard for him to find his way back to us.

"You should have asked the kaffirs," one of our number said with a laugh. "All the kaffirs know our veldkornet."

But Floris did not speak about what happened that night, when we saw him riding out under the starlight, following after his son and shouting to him to be a man and to fight for his country. Also, Floris did not mention Stephanus again, his son who was not worthy to be a Van Barnevelt.

After that we got separated. Our veldkornet was the first to be taken prisoner. And I often felt that he must feel very lonely on St. Helena. Because there were no kaffirs from whom he could ask the way out of the barbed-wire camp.

Then, at last our leaders came together at Vereeniging, and peace was made. And we returned to our farms, relieved that the war was over, but with heavy hearts at the thought that it had all been for nothing and that over the Transvaal the Vierkleur would not wave again.

And Floris van Barnevelt put back in its place, on the wall of the voorkamer, the copy of his family tree that had been carried with him in his knapsack throughout the war. Then a new schoolmaster came to this part of the Marico, and after a long talk with Floris, the schoolmaster wrote behind Stephanus's name, between two curved lines, the two words that you can still read there: "Obiit Mafeking."

Consequently, if you ask any person hereabouts what "obiit" means, he is able to tell you, right away, that it is a foreign word, and that it means to ride up to the English, holding your Mauser in the air, with a white flag tied to it, near the muzzle.

But it was long afterwards that Floris van Barnevelt started telling his story.

And then they took no notice of him. And they wouldn't allow him to be nominated for the Drogevlei School Committee on the grounds that a man must be wrong in the head to talk in such an irresponsible fashion.

But I knew that Floris had a good story, and that its only fault was that he told it badly. He mentioned the Drogevlei School Committee too soon. And he knocked the ash out of his pipe in the wrong place. And he always insisted on telling that part of the story that he should have left out.

The Love Potion

You mention the juba-plant (Oom Schalk Lourens said). Oh, yes, everybody in the Marico knows about the juba-plant. It grows high up on the krantzes, and they say you must pick off one of its little red berries at midnight, under the full moon. Then, if you are a young man, and you are anxious for a girl to fall in love with you, all you have to do is to squeeze the juice of the juba-berry into her coffee.

They say that after the girl has drunk the juba-juice she begins to forget all sorts of things. She forgets that your forehead is rather low, and that your ears stick out, and that your mouth is too big. She even forgets having told you, the week before last, that she wouldn't marry you if you were the only man in the Transvaal.

All she knows is that the man she gazes at, over her empty coffee-cup, has grown remarkably handsome. You can see from this that the plant must be very potent in its effects. I mean, if you consider what some of the men in the Marico look like.

One young man I knew, however, was not very enthusiastic about juba-juice. In fact, he always said that before he climbed up the krantz one night, to pick one of those red berries, he was more popular with the girls than he was afterwards. This young man said that his decline in favour with the girls of the neighbourhood might perhaps be due to the fact that, shortly after he had picked the juba-berry, he lost most of his front teeth.

This happened when the girl's father, who was an irascible sort of fellow, caught the young man in the act of squeezing juba-juice into his daughter's cup.

And afterwards, while others talked of the magic properties of this love potion, the young man would listen in silence, and his lip would curl in a sneer over the place where his front teeth used to be.

"Yes, kêrels," he would lisp at the end, "I suppose I must have picked that juba-berry at the wrong time. Perhaps the moon wasn't full enough, or something. Or perhaps it wasn't just exactly midnight. I am only glad now that I didn't pick off two of those red berries while I was about it."

We all felt it was a sad thing that the juba-plant had done to that young man.

But with Gideon van der Merwe it was different.

One night I was out shooting in the veld with a lamp fastened on my hat. You know that kind of shooting: in the glare of the lamp-light you can see only the eyes of the thing you are aiming at, and you get three months if you are caught. They made it illegal to hunt by lamp-light since the time a policeman got shot in the foot, this way, when he was out tracking cattle-smugglers on the Bechuanaland border.

The magistrate at Zeerust, who did not know the ways of the cattle-smugglers, found that the shooting was an accident. This verdict satisfied everybody except the policeman, whose foot was still bandaged when he came into court. But the men in the Volksraad, some of whom had been cattle-smugglers themselves, knew better than the magistrate did as to how the policeman came to have a couple of buckshot in the soft part of his foot, and accordingly they brought in this new law.

Therefore I walked very quietly that night on the krantz.

Frequently I put out my light and stood very still amongst the trees, and waited long moments to make sure I was not being followed. Ordinarily, there would have been little to fear, but a couple of days before two policemen had been seen disappearing into the bush. By their looks they seemed young policemen, who were anxious for promotion, and who didn't know that it is more becoming for a policeman to drink an honest farmer's peach brandy than to arrest him for hunting by lamp-light.

I was walking along, turning the light from side to side, when suddenly, about a hundred paces from me, in the full brightness of the lamp, I saw a pair of eyes. When I also saw, above the eyes, a policeman's khaki helmet, I remembered that a moonlight night, such as that was, was not good for finding buck.

So I went home.

I took the shortest way, too, which was over the side of the krantz – the steep side – and on my way down I clutched at a variety of branches, tree-roots, stone ledges and tufts of grass. Later on, at the foot of the krantz, when I came to and was able to sit up, there was that policeman bending over me.

"Oom Schalk," he said, "I was wondering if you would lend me your lamp."

I looked up. It was Gideon van der Merwe, the young policeman who had been stationed for some time at Derdepoort. I had met him on several occasions and had found him very likeable.

"You can have my lamp," I answered, "but you must be careful. It's worse for a policeman to get caught breaking the law than for an ordinary man."

Gideon van der Merwe shook his head.

"No, I don't want to go shooting with the lamp," he said, "I want to – "

And then he paused.

He laughed nervously.

"It seems silly to say it, Oom Schalk," he said, "but perhaps you'll understand. I have come to look for a juba-plant. I need it for my studies. For my third-class sergeant's examination. And it will soon be midnight, and I can't find one of those plants anywhere."

I felt sorry for Gideon. It struck me that he would never make a good policeman. If he couldn't find a juba-plant, of which there were thousands on the krantz, it would be much harder for him to find the spoor of a cattle-smuggler.

So I handed him my lamp and explained where he had to go and look. Gideon thanked me and walked off.

About half an hour later he was back.

He took a red berry out of his tunic pocket and showed it to me. For fear he should tell any more lies about needing that juba-berry for his studies, I spoke first.

"Lettie Cordier?" I asked.

Gideon nodded. He was very shy, though, and wouldn't talk much at the start. But I had guessed long ago that Gideon van der Merwe was not calling at Krisjan Cordier's house so often just to hear Krisjan relate the story of his life.

Nevertheless, I mentioned Krisjan Cordier's life-story.

"Yes," Gideon replied, "Lettie's father has got up to what he was like at the age of seven. It has taken him a month, so far."

"He must be glad to get you to listen," I said, "the only other man who listened for any length of time was an insurance agent. But he left after a fortnight. By that time Krisjan had reached to only a little beyond his fifth birthday."

"But Lettie is wonderful, Oom Schalk," Gideon went on. "I have never spoken more than a dozen words to her. And, of course, it is ridiculous to expect her even to look at a policeman. But to sit there, in the voorkamer, with her father talking about all the things he could do before he was six – and Lettie coming in now and again with more coffee – that is love, Oom Schalk."

I agreed with him that it must be.

"I have worked it out," Gideon explained, "that at the rate he is going now, Lettie's father will have come to the end of his life-story in two years' time, and after that I won't have any excuse for going there. That worries me."

I said that no doubt it was disconcerting.

"I have tried often to tell Lettie how much I think of her," Gideon said, "but every time, as soon as I start, I get a foolish feeling. My uniform begins to look shabby. My boots seem to curl up at the toes. And my voice gets shaky, and all I can say to her is that I will come round again, soon, as I have simply got to hear the rest of her father's life-story."

"Then what is your idea with the juba-juice?" I asked.

"The juba-juice," Gideon van der Merwe said, wistfully, "might make her say something first."

We parted shortly afterwards. I took up my lamp and gun, and as I saw Gideon's figure disappear among the trees I thought of what a good fellow he was. And very simple. Still, he was best off as a policeman, I reflected. For if he was a cattle-smuggler it seemed to me that he would get arrested every time he tried to cross the border.

Next morning I rode over to Krisjan Cordier's farm to remind him about the tin of sheep-dip that he still owed me from the last dipping season.

As I stayed for only about an hour, I wasn't able to get in a word about the sheep-dip, but Krisjan managed to tell me quite a lot about the things he did at the age of nine. When Lettie came in with the coffee I made a casual remark to her father about Gideon van der Merwe.

"Oh, yes, he's an interesting young man," Krisjan Cordier said, "and very intelligent. It is a pleasure for me to relate to him the story of my life. He says the incidents I describe to him are not only thrilling, but very helpful. I can quite understand that. I wouldn't be surprised if he is made a sergeant one of these days. For these reasons I always dwell on the more helpful parts of my story."

I didn't take much notice of Krisjan's remarks, however. Instead, I looked carefully at Lettie when I mentioned Gideon's name. She didn't give much away, but I am quick at these things, and I saw enough. The colour that crept into her cheeks. The light that came in her eyes.

On my way back I encountered Lettie. She was standing under a thorn-tree. With her brown arms and her sweet, quiet face and her full bosom, she was a very pretty picture. There was no doubt that Lettie Cordier would make a fine wife for any man. It wasn't hard to understand Gideon's feelings about her.

"Lettie," I asked, "do you love him?"

"I love him, Oom Schalk," she answered.

It was as simple as that.

Lettie guessed I meant Gideon van der Merwe, without my having spoken his name. Accordingly, it was easy for me to acquaint Lettie with what had happened the night before, on the krantz, in the moonlight. At least, I only told her the parts that mattered to her, such as the way I explained to Gideon where the juba-plant grew. Another man might have wearied her with a long and unnecessary description of the way he fell down the krantz, clutching at branches and tree-roots. But I am different. I told her that it was Gideon who fell down the krantz.

After all, it was Lettie's and Gideon's love affair, and I didn't want to bring myself into it too much.

"Now you'll know what to do, Lettie," I said. "Put your coffee on the table within easy reach of Gideon. Then give him what you think is long enough to squeeze the juba-juice into your cup."

"Perhaps it will be even better," Lettie said, "if I watch through a crack in the door."

I patted her head approvingly.

"After that you come into the voorkamer and drink your coffee," I said.

"Yes, Oom Schalk," she answered simply.

"And when you have drunk the coffee," I concluded, "you'll know what to do next. Only don't go too far."

It was pleasant to see the warm blood mount to her face. As I rode off I said to myself that Gideon van der Merwe was a lucky fellow.

There isn't much more to tell about Lettie and Gideon.

When I saw Gideon some time afterwards, he was very elated, as I had expected he would be.

"So the juba-plant worked?" I enquired.

"It was wonderful, Oom Schalk," Gideon answered, "and the funny part of it was that Lettie's father was not there, either, when I put the juba-juice into her coffee. Lettie had brought him a message, just before then, that he was wanted in the mealie-lands."

"And was the juba-juice all they claim for it?" I asked.

"You'd be surprised how quickly it acted," he said. "Lettie just took one sip at the coffee and then jumped straight on to my lap."

But then Gideon van der Merwe winked in a way that made me believe that he was not so very simple, after all.

"I was pretty certain that the juba-juice would work, Oom Schalk," he said, "after Lettie's father told me that you had been there that morning."

Makapan's Caves

K AFFIRS? (said Oom Schalk Lourens). Yes, I know them. And they're all the same. I fear the Almighty, and I respect His works, but I could never understand why He made the kaffir and the rinderpest. The Hottentot is a little better. The Hottentot will only steal the biltong hanging out on the line to dry. He won't steal the line as well. That is where the kaffir is different.

Still, sometimes you come across a good kaffir, who is faithful and upright and a true Christian and doesn't let the wild-dogs catch the sheep. I always think that it isn't right to kill that kind of kaffir.

I remember about one kaffir we had, by the name of Nongaas. How we got him was after this fashion. It was in the year of the big drought, when there was no grass, and the water in the pan had dried up. Our cattle died like flies. It was terrible. Every day ten or twelve or twenty died. So my father said we must pack everything on the wagons and trek up to the Dwarsberge, where he heard there had been good rains. I was six years old, then, the youngest in the family. Most of the time I sat in the back of the wagon, with my mother and my two sisters. My brother Hendrik was seventeen, and he helped my father and the kaffirs to drive on our cattle. That was how we trekked. Many more of our cattle died along the way, but after about two months we got into the Lowveld and my father said that God had been good to us. For the grass was green along the Dwarsberge.

One morning we came to some kaffir huts, where my father bartered two sacks of mealies for a roll of tobacco. A piccanin of about my own age was standing in front of a hut, and he looked at us all the time and grinned. But mostly he looked at my brother Hendrik. And that was not a wonder, either. Even in those days my brother Hendrik was careful about his appearance, and he always tried to be fashionably dressed. On Sundays he even wore socks. When we had loaded up the mealies, my father cut off a plug of Boer tobacco and gave it to the piccanin, who grinned still more, so that we saw every one of his teeth, which were very white. He put the plug in his mouth and bit it. Then we all laughed. The piccanin looked just like a puppy that has swallowed a piece of meat, and turns his head sideways, to see how it tastes.

That was in the morning. We went right on until the afternoon, for my father wanted to reach Tweekoppiesfontein, where we were going to stand with our cattle for some time. It was late in the afternoon when we got there, and we started to outspan. Just as I was getting off the wagon, I looked round and saw something jumping quickly behind a bush. It looked like some animal, so I was afraid, and told my brother Hendrik, who took up his gun and walked slowly towards the bush. We saw, directly afterwards, that it was the piccanin whom we had seen that morning in front of the hut. He must have been following behind our wagons for about ten miles. He looked dirty and tired, but when my brother went up to him he began to grin again, and seemed very happy. We didn't know what to do with him, so Hendrik shouted to him to go home, and started throwing stones at him. But my father was a merciful man, and after he had heard Nongaas's story – for that was the name of the piccanin – he said he could stay with us, but he must be good, and not tell lies and steal, like the other kaffirs. Nongaas told us in the Sechuana language, which my father understood, that his father and mother had been killed by the lions, and that he was living with his uncle, whom he didn't like, but that he liked my brother Hendrik, and that was why he had followed our wagons.

Nongaas remained with us for many years. He grew up with us. He was a very good kaffir, and as time went by he became much attached to all of us. But he worshipped my brother Hendrik. As he grew older, my father sometimes spoke to Nongaas about his soul, and explained to him about God. But although he told my father that he understood, I could see that whenever Nongaas thought of God, he was really only thinking of Hendrik.

It was just after my twenty-first birthday that we got news that Hermanus Potgieter and his whole family had been killed by a kaffir tribe under Makapan. They also said that, after killing him, the kaffirs stripped off old Potgieter's skin and made wallets out of it in which to carry their dagga. It was very wicked of the kaffirs to have done that, especially as dagga makes you mad and it is a sin to smoke it. A commando was called up from our district to go and attack the tribe and teach them to have respect for the white man's laws – and above all, to have more respect for the white man's skin. My mother and sisters baked a great deal of harde beskuit, which we packed up, together with mealie-meal and biltong. We also took out the lead mould and melted bullets. The next morning my brother and I set out on horseback for Makapan's kraal. We were accompanied by Nongaas, whom we took along with us to look after the horses and light the fires. My father stayed at home. He said that he was too old to go on commando, unless it was to fight the redcoats, if there were still any left.

But he gave us some good advice.

"Don't forget to read your Bible, my sons," he called out as we rode away. "Pray the Lord to help you, and when you shoot always aim for the stomach." These remarks were typical of my father's deeply religious nature, and he also knew that it was easier to hit a man in the stomach than in the head: and it is just as good, because no man can live long after his intestines have been shot away.

Well, we rode on, my brother and I, with Nongaas following a few yards behind us on the pack-horse. Now and again we fell in with other burghers, many of whom brought their wagons with them, until, on the third day, we reached Makapan's kraal, where the big commando had already gone into camp. We got there in the evening, and everywhere as far as we could see there were fires burning in a big circle. There were over two hundred wagons, and on their tents the fires shone red and yellow. We reported ourselves to the veldkornet, who showed us a place where we could camp, next to the four Van Rensburg brothers. Nongaas had just made the fire and boiled the coffee when one of the Van Rensburgs came up and invited us over to their wagon. They had shot a rietbok and were roasting pieces of it on the coals.

We all shook hands and said it was good weather for the mealies if only the ruspes didn't eat them, and that it was time we had another president, and that rietbok tasted very fine when roasted on the coals. Then they told us what had happened about the kaffirs. Makapan and his followers had seen the commandos coming from a distance, and after firing a few shots at them had all fled into the caves in the krantz. These caves stretched away underground very far and with many turnings. So, as the Boers could not storm the kaffirs without losing heavily, the kommandant gave instructions that the ridge was to be surrounded and the kaffirs starved out. They were all inside the caves, the whole tribe, men, women and children. They had already been there six days, and as they couldn't have much food left, and as there was only a small dam with brackish water, we were hopeful of being able to kill off most of the kaffirs without wasting ammunition.

Already, when the wind blew towards us from the mouth of the caves, the stink was terrible. We would have pitched our camp further back, only that we were afraid some of the kaffirs would escape between the fires.

The following morning I saw for the first time why we couldn't drive the kaffirs from their lairs, even though our commando was four hundred strong. All over, through the rocks and bushes, I could see black openings in the krantz, that led right into the deep parts of the earth. Here and there we could see dead bodies lying. But there were still left a lot of kaffirs that were not dead, and them we could not see. But they had guns, which they had bought from the illicit traders and the missionaries, and they shot at us whenever we came within range. And all the time there was that stench of decaying bodies.

For another week the siege went on. Then we heard that our leaders, Marthinus Wessels Pretorius and Paul Kruger, had quarrelled. Kruger wanted to attack the kaffirs immediately and finish the affair, but Pretorius said it was too dangerous and he didn't want any more burghers killed. He said that already the hand of the Lord lay heavy upon Makapan, and in another few weeks the kaffirs would all be dead of starvation. But Paul Kruger said that it would even be better if the hand of the Lord lay still heavier upon the kaffirs. Eventually Paul Kruger obtained permission to take fifty volunteers and storm the caves from one side, while Kommandant Piet Potgieter was to advance from the other side with two hundred men, to distract the attention of the kaffirs. Kruger was popular with all of us, and nearly everyone volunteered to go with him. So he picked fifty men, among whom were the Van Rensburgs and my brother. Therefore, as I did not want to stay behind and guard the camp, I had to join Piet Potgieter's commando.

All the preparations were made, and the following morning we got ready to attack. My brother Hendrik was very proud and happy at having been chosen for the more dangerous part. He oiled his gun very carefully and polished up his veldskoens.

Then Nongaas came up and I noticed that he looked very miserable.

"My baas," he said to my brother Hendrik, "you mustn't go and fight. They'll shoot you dead."

My brother shook his head.

"Then let me go with you, baas," Nongaas said; "I will go in front and look after you."

Hendrik only laughed.

"Look here, Nongaas," he said, "you can stay behind and cook the dinner. I will get back in time to eat it."

The whole commando came together and we all knelt down and prayed. Then Marthinus Wessels Pretorius said we must sing Hymn Number 23, "Rest my soul, thy God is king." Furthermore, we sang another hymn and also a psalm. Most people would have thought that one hymn would be enough. But not so Pretorius. He always made quite sure of everything he did. Then we moved off to the attack. We fought bravely, but the kaffirs were many, and they lay in the darkness of the caves, and shot at us without our being able to see them. While the fighting lasted it was worse than the lyddite bombs at Paardeberg. And the stench was terrible. We tied handkerchiefs round the lower part of our face, but that did not help. Also, since we were not Englishmen, many of us had no handkerchiefs. Still we fought on, shooting at an enemy we could not see. We rushed right up to the mouth of one of the caves, and even got some distance into it, when our leader, Kommandant Piet Potgieter, flung up his hands and fell backwards, shot through the breast. We carried him out, but he was quite dead. So we lost heart and retired.

When we returned from the fight we found that the other attacking party had also been defeated. They had shot many kaffirs, but there were still hundreds of them left, who fought all the more fiercely with hunger gnawing at their bellies.

I went back to our camp. There was only Nongaas, sitting forward on a stone, with his face on his arms. An awful fear clutched me as I asked him what was wrong.

"Baas Hendrik," he replied, and as he looked at me in his eyes there was much sorrow, "Baas Hendrik did not come back."

I went out immediately and made enquiries, but nobody could tell me anything for sure. They remembered quite well seeing my brother Hendrik when they stormed the cave. He was right in amongst the foremost of the attackers. When I heard that, I felt a great pride in my brother, although I also knew that nothing else could be expected of the son of my father. But no man could tell me what had happened to him. All they knew was that when they got back he was not amongst them.

I spoke to Marthinus Wessels Pretorius and asked him to send out another party to seek for my brother. But Pretorius was angry.

"I will not allow one more man," he replied. "It was all Kruger's doing. I was against it from the start. Now Kommandant Potgieter has been killed, who was a better man than Kruger and all his Dopper clique put together. If any man goes back to the caves I shall discharge him from the commando."

But I don't think it was right of Pretorius. Because Paul Kruger was only trying to do his duty, and afterwards, when he was nominated for president, I voted for him.

It was eleven o'clock when I again reached our part of the laager. Nongaas was still sitting on the flat stone, and I saw that he had carried out my brother Hendrik's instructions, and that the pot was boiling on the fire. The dinner was ready, but my brother was not there. That sight was too much for me, and I went and lay down alone under the Van Rensburgs' wagon.

I looked up again, about half an hour later, and I saw Nongaas walking away with a water-bottle and a small sack strapped to his back. He said nothing to me, but I knew he was going to look for my brother Hendrik. Nongaas knew that if his baas was still alive he would need him. So he went to him. That was all. For a long while I watched Nongaas as he crept along through the rocks and bushes. I supposed it was his intention to lie in wait near one of the caves and then crawl inside when the night came. That was a very brave thing to do. If Makapan's kaffirs saw him they would be sure to kill him, because he was helping the Boers against them, and also because he was a Bechuana.

The evening came, but neither my brother Hendrik nor Nongaas. All that night I sat with my face to the caves and never slept. Then in the morning I got up and loaded my gun. I said to myself that if Nongaas had been killed in the attempt there was only one thing left for me to do. I myself must go to my brother.

I walked out first into the veld, in case one of the officers saw me and made me come back. Then I walked along the ridge and got under cover of the bushes. From there I crawled along, hiding in the long grass and behind the stones, so that I came to one part of Makapan's stronghold where things were more quiet. I got to within about two hundred yards of a cave. There I lay very still, behind a big rock, to find out if there were any kaffirs watching from that side. Occasionally I heard the sound of a shot being fired, but that was far away.

Afterwards I fell asleep, for I was very weary with the anxiety and through not having slept the night before.

When I woke up the sun was right overhead. It was hot and there were no clouds in the sky. Only there were a few aasvoëls, which flew round and round very slowly, without ever seeming to flap their wings. Now and again one of them would fly down and settle on the ground, and it was very horrible. I thought of my brother Hendrik and shivered. I looked towards the cave. Inside it seemed as though there was something moving. A minute later I saw that it was a kaffir coming stealthily towards the entrance. He appeared to be looking in my direction, and for fear that he should see me and call the other kaffirs, I jumped up quickly and shot at him, aiming at the stomach. He fell over like a sack of potatoes and I was thankful for my father's advice. But I had to act quickly. If the other kaffirs had heard the shot they would all come running up at once. And I didn't want that to happen. I didn't like the look of those aasvoëls. So I decided to take a great risk. Accordingly I ran as fast as I could towards the cave and rushed right into it, so that, even if the kaffirs did come, they wouldn't see me amongst the shadows. For a long time I lay down and waited. But as no more kaffirs came, I got up and walked slowly down a dark passage, looking round every time to see that nobody followed me, and to make sure that I would find my way back. For there were many twists and turnings, and the whole krantz seemed to be hollowed out.

I knew that my search would be very difficult. But there was something that seemed to tell me that my brother was nearby. So I was strong in my faith, and I knew that the Lord would lead me aright. And I found my brother Hendrik, and he was alive. It was with a feeling of great joy that I came across him. I saw him in the dim light that came through a big split in the roof. He was lying against a boulder, holding his leg and groaning. I saw afterwards that his leg was sprained and much swollen, but that was all that was wrong. So great was my brother Hendrik's surprise at seeing me that at first he could not talk. He just held my hand and laughed softly, and when I touched his forehead I knew he was feverish. I gave him some brandy out of my flask, and in a few words he told me all that had happened. When they stormed the cave he was right in front and as the kaffirs retreated he followed them up. But they all ran in different ways, until my brother found himself alone. He tried to get back, but lost his way and fell down a dip. In that way he sprained his ankle so severely that he had been in agony all the time. He crawled into a far corner and remained there, with the danger and the darkness and his pain. But the worst of all was the stink of the rotting bodies.

"Then Nongaas came," my brother Hendrik said.

"Nongaas?" I asked him.

"Yes," he replied. "He found me and gave me food and water, and carried me on his back. Then the water gave out and I was very thirsty. So Nongaas took the bottle to go and fill it at the pan. But it is very dangerous to get there, and I am so frightened they may kill him."

"They will not kill him," I said. "Nongaas will come back." I said that, but in my heart I was afraid. For the caves were many and dark, and the kaffirs were blood-mad. It would not do to wait. So I lifted Hendrik on my shoulder and carried him towards the entrance. He was in much pain.

"You know," he whispered, "Nongaas was crying when he found me. He thought I was dead. He has been very good to me – so very good. Do you remember that day when he followed behind our wagons? He looked so very trustful and so little, and yet I – I threw stones at him. I wish I did not do that. I only hope that he comes back safe. He was crying and stroking my hair."

As I said, my brother Hendrik was feverish.

"Of course he will come back," I answered him. But this time I knew that I lied. For as I came through the mouth of the cave I kicked against the kaffir I had shot there. The body sagged over to one side and I saw the face.

Yellow Moepels

IF ever you spoke to my father about witch-doctors (Oom Schalk Lourens said), he would always relate one story. And at the end of it he would explain that, while a witch-doctor could foretell the future for you from the bones, at the same time he could only tell you the things that didn't matter. My father used to say that the important things were as much hidden from the witch-doctor as from the man who listened to his prophecy.

My father said that when he was sixteen he went with his friend, Paul, a stripling of about his own age, to a kaffir witch-doctor. They had heard that this witch-doctor was very good at throwing the bones.

This witch-doctor lived alone in a mud hut. While they were still on the way to the hut the two youths laughed and jested, but as soon as they got inside they felt different. They were impressed. The witch-doctor was very old and very wrinkled. He had on a queer head-dress made up from the tails of different wild animals.

You could tell that the boys were overawed as they sat there on the floor in the dark. Because my father, who had meant to hand the witch-doctor only a plug of Boer tobacco, gave him a whole roll. And Paul, who had said, when they were outside, that he was going to give him nothing at all, actually handed over his hunting knife.

Then he threw the bones. He threw first for my father. He told him many things. He told him that he would grow up to be a good burgher, and that he would one day be very prosperous. He would have a big farm and many cattle and two ox-wagons.

But what the witch-doctor did not tell my father was that in years to come he would have a son, Schalk, who could tell better stories than any man in the Marico.

Then the witch-doctor threw the bones for Paul. For a long while he was silent. He looked from the bones to Paul, and back to the bones, in a strange way. Then he spoke.

"I can see you go far away, my kleinbaas," he said, "very far away over the great waters. Away from your own land, my kleinbaas."

"And the veld," Paul asked, "and the krantzes and the vlaktes?"

"And away from your own people," the witch-doctor said.

"And will I – will I – "

"No, my kleinbasie," the witch-doctor answered, "you will not come back. You will die there."

My father said that when they came out of that hut Paul Kruger's face was very white. That was why my father used to say that, while a witch-doctor could tell you true things, he could not tell you the things that really mattered.

And my father was right.

Take the case of Neels Potgieter and Martha Rossouw, for instance. They became engaged to be married just before the affair at Paarde-kraal. There, on the hoogte, our leaders pointed out to us that, although the Transvaal had been annexed by Sir Theophilus Shepstone, it never-theless meant that we would have to go on paying taxes just the same. Everybody knew then that it was war.

Neels Potgieter and I were in the same commando.

It was arranged that the burghers of the neighbourhood should assemble at the veldkornet's house. Instructions had also been given that no women were to be present. There was much fighting to be done, and this final leave-taking was likely to be an embarrassing thing.

Nevertheless, as always, the women came. And among them was Neels's sweetheart, Martha Rossouw. And also there was my sister, Annie.

I shall never forget that scene in front of the veldkornet's house, in the early morning, when there were still shadows on the rante, and a thin wind blew through the grass. We had no predikant there; but an ouder-ling, with two bandoliers slung across his body, and a Martini in his hand, said a few words. He was a strong and simple man, with no great gifts of oratory. But when he spoke about the Transvaal we could feel what was in his heart, and we took off our hats in silence.

And it was not long afterwards that I again took off my hat in much the same way. Then it was at Majuba Hill. It was after the battle, and the ouderling still had his two bandoliers around him when we buried him at the foot of the koppie.

But what impressed me most was the prayer that followed the ou-derling's brief address. In front of the veldkornet's house we knelt, each burgher with his rifle at his side. And the womenfolk knelt down with us. And the wind seemed very gentle as it stirred the tall grass-blades; very gentle as it swept over the bared heads of the men and fluttered the kappies and skirts of the women; very gentle as it carried the prayers of our nation over the veld.

After that we stood up and sang a hymn. The ceremony was over. The agterryers brought us our horses. And, dry-eyed and tight-lipped, each woman sent her man forth to war. There was no weeping.

Then, in accordance with Boer custom, we fired a volley into the air.

"Voorwaarts, burghers," came the veldkornet's order, and we cantered down the road in twos. But before we left I had overheard Neels Potgieter say something to Martha Rossouw as he leant out of the saddle and kissed her. My sister Annie, standing beside my horse, also heard.

"When the moepels are ripe, Martha," Neels said, "I will come to you again."

Annie and I looked at each other and smiled. It was a pretty thing that Neels had said. But then Martha was also pretty. More pretty than the veld-trees that bore those yellow moepels, I reflected – and more wild.

I was still thinking of this when our commando had passed over the bult, in a long line, on our way to the south, where Natal was, and the other commandos, and Majuba.

This was the war of Bronkhorstspruit and General Colley and Laing's Nek. You have no doubt heard many accounts of this war, some of them truthful, perhaps. For it is a singular thing that, as a man grows older, and looks back on fights that he has been in, he keeps on remembering, each year, more and more of the enemy that he has shot.

Klaas Uys was a man like that. Each year, on his birthday, he remembered one or two more redcoats that he had shot, whereupon he got up straight away and put another few notches in the wood part of his rifle, along the barrel. And he said his memory was getting better every year.

All the time I was on commando, I received only one letter. That came from Annie, my sister. She said I was not to take any risks, and that I must keep far away from the English, especially if they had guns. She also said I was to remember that I was a white man, and that if there was any dangerous work to be done, I had to send a kaffir out to do it.

There were more things like that in Annie's letter. But I had no need of her advice. Our kommandant was a God-fearing and wily man, and he knew even better ways than Annie did for keeping out of range of the enemy's fire.

But Annie also said, at the end of her letter, that she and Martha Rossouw had gone to a witch-doctor. They had gone to find out about Neels Potgieter and me. Now, if I had been at home, I would not have permitted Annie to indulge in this nonsense.

Especially as the witch-doctor said to her, "Yes, missus, I can see Baas Schalk Lourens. He will come back safe. He is very clever, Baas Schalk. He lies behind a big stone, with a dirty brown blanket pulled over his head. And he stays behind that stone until the fighting is finished – quite finished."

According to Annie's letter, the witch-doctor told her a few other things about me, too. But I won't bother to repeat them now. I think I have said enough to show you what sort of a scoundrel that old kaffir was. He not only took advantage of the credulity of a simple girl, but he also tried to be funny at the expense of a young man who was fighting for his country's freedom.

What was more, Annie said that she had recognised it was me right away, just from the kaffir's description of that blanket.

To Martha Rossouw the witch-doctor said, "Baas Neels Potgieter will come back to you, missus, when the moepels are ripe again. At sun-under he will come."

That was all he said about Neels, and there wasn't very much in that, anyway, seeing that Neels himself – except for the bit about the sunset – had made the very same prophecy the day the commando set out. I suppose that witch-doctor had been too busy thinking out foolish and spiteful things about me to be able to give any attention to Neels Potgieter's affairs.

But I didn't mention Annie's letter to Neels. He might have wanted to know more than I was willing to tell him. More, even, perhaps, than Martha was willing to tell him – Martha of the wild heart.

Then, at last, the war ended, and over the Transvaal the Vierkleur waved again. And the commandos went home by their different ways. And our leaders revived their old quarrels as to who should be president. And, everywhere, except for a number of lonely graves on hillside and vlakte, things were as they had been before Shepstone came.

It was getting on towards evening when our small band rode over the bult again, and once more came to a halt at the veldkornet's house. A messenger had been sent on in advance to announce our coming, and from far around the women and children and old men had gathered to welcome their victorious burghers back from the war. And there were tears in many eyes when we sang, "Hef, Burghers, Hef."

And the moepels were ripe and yellow on the trees.

And in the dusk Neels Potgieter found Martha Rossouw and kissed her. At sundown, as the witch-doctor had said. But there was one important thing that the witch-doctor had not told. It was something that Neels Potgieter did not know, either, just then. And that was that Martha did not want him any more.

Bechuana Interlude

WHEN I last saw Lenie Venter – Oom Schalk Lourens said – she was sitting in the voorkamer of her parents' farmhouse at Koedoesrand, drawing small circles on the blotting-paper. And I didn't know whether I had to be sorry for Lenie. Or for Johnny de Clerk. Or for Gert Oosthuizen. Or perhaps for the kaffir schoolmaster at Ramoutsa.

Of course, Lenie had learnt this trick of drawing circles from Johnny de Clerk, the young insurance agent. She had watched him, very intently, the first time he had called on Piet Venter. He had been in the Marico for some time, but this was his first visit to Koedoesrand. Johnny de Clerk looked very elegant, in his blue suit with the short jacket and the wide trousers, and while he sat with a lot of printed documents in front of him, talking about the advantages of being insured, he drew lots of small circles on the blotting-paper.

I was going by mule-cart to the Bechuanaland Protectorate, and on my way I had stopped at Piet Venter's house for a cup of coffee, and to ask him if there was anything I could order for him from the Indian store at Ramoutsa. But he said there wasn't.

"What about a drum of cattle-dip?" I hinted, remembering that Piet still owed me five gallons of dip.

"No," he answered. "I don't need cattle-dip now."

"Perhaps I can order you a few rolls of barbed wire," I suggested. This time I was thinking of the wire he had borrowed from me for his new sheep-camp.

"No, thank you," he said politely, "I don't need barbed wire, either." Piet Venter was funny, that way.

I was on the point of leaving, when Johnny de Clerk came in, very smart in his blue suit and his light felt hat and his pointed shoes. He introduced himself, and we all sat down and chatted very affably for a while. Afterwards Johnny took out a number of insurance forms, and said things to Piet Venter about a thousand pound policy, speaking very fast. From the way Johnny de Clerk kept on looking sideways at me, while he talked, I gathered that my presence was disturbing him, and that he couldn't talk his best while there was a third party listening.

So I lit my pipe and stayed longer.

I noticed that Lenie kept flitting in and out of the voorkamer, with bright eyes and red cheeks. I also noticed that, soon after Johnny de Clerk's arrival, she had gone into the bedroom for a few minutes and had come out wearing a new pink frock. Lenie was pretty enough to make any man feel flattered if he knew that she had gone into the bedroom and put on a new pink frock just because he was there. She had dark hair and dark eyes, and when she smiled you could see that her teeth were very white.

Her sudden interest in this young insurance agent struck me as being all the more singular, because everybody in the Marico knew that Lenie was being courted by Gert Oosthuizen.

But it seemed that Johnny de Clerk had not noticed Lenie's blushes and her new frock. He appeared very unobservant about these things. It did not seem right that a young girl's efforts at attracting a man should be wasted in that fashion. That was another reason why I went on sitting there while the insurance agent talked to Piet Venter. I even went so far as to cough, once or twice, when Johnny de Clerk mentioned the amount of the policy that he thought Piet Venter should take out.

When he had filled the whole sheet of blotting-paper with small circles, Johnny de Clerk stopped talking and put the printed documents in order.

"I have proved to you why you should be insured for a thousand pounds, Oom Piet," he said, "so just sign your name here."

Piet Venter shook his head.

"Oh no," he replied, "I don't want to."

"But you must," Johnny de Clerk went on, waving his hand towards Lenie, without looking up, "for the sake of your wife, here, you must."

"That is not my wife," Piet Venter replied, "that's my daughter, Lenie. My wife has gone to Zeerust to visit her sister."

"Well, then, for the sake of your wife and daughter, Lenie," Johnny de Clerk said, "and what's more, I've already spent an hour talking to you. If I spend another hour I shall have to insure you for two thousand pounds."

Piet Venter got frightened then, and took off his jacket and signed the application form without any more fuss. By the way he passed his hand over his forehead I could see he was pleased to have got out of it so easily. I thought it was very considerate of Johnny de Clerk to have warned him in time. A more dishonest insurance agent, I felt, would just have gone on sitting there for the full two hours, and would then have filled in the documents, very coolly, for two thousand pounds. It was a pleasure for me to see an honest insurance agent at work, after I had come across so many of what you can call the dishonest kind.

Johnny de Clerk went out then, with the papers, saying that he would call again.

I left shortly afterwards.

"By the way," I said to Piet Venter, as I took up my hat, "perhaps I could order another trek-chain for you at Ramoutsa. It's always useful to have two trek-chains."

Piet Venter thought deeply for a few moments.

"No, Schalk, it's no good," he said, slowly. "If a man has got a spare trek-chain, people always want to borrow it."

I wondered much about Piet Venter as I walked out to the mule-cart.

I had just unfastened the reins from the front wheel, and was getting ready to drive away, when I heard light footsteps running across the grass. I looked round. It was Lenie. She looked very pretty running like that, with her eyes shining and her dark hair flying in the wind.

She had been running fast. The breath came in short gasps from between her parted lips. The sun shone very white on her small teeth.

Lenie was too excited at first to talk. She leant against the side of the cart, panting. I was glad she hadn't taken it into her mind to lean up against one of the mules, instead.

At last she found her voice.

"I have just remembered, Oom Schalk," she said, "we have run out of blotting-paper. Will you please get me a few sheets from Ramoutsa?"

"Yes, certainly, Lenie," I replied, "yes, of course. Blotting-paper. Oh, yes, for sure. Blotting-paper."

I spoke to her in that way, tactfully, to make it appear as though it was quite an ordinary thing she had asked me to get. And I said other things that were even more tactful.

She smiled when I spoke like that. And I remembered her smile for most of the way to Ramoutsa. It was an uneasy sort of smile.

The usual small crowd of farmers from different parts of the Marico were hanging around the Indian store when I got there. After making their purchases they whiled away the time in discussing politics and the mealie-crops and the miltsiekte. They stood there, talking, to give their mules a chance to rest. Sometimes a mule got sunstroke, from resting for such a long time in the sun, while his owner was talking.

I ordered the things I wanted. The Indian wrote them all down in a book, and then got one of his kaffirs to carry them out to my mule-cart.

"By the way," I said, clearing my throat, and trying to speak as though I had just remembered something, "I also want blotting-paper. Six sheets will do."

The Indian looked in my eyes and nodded his head up and down, several times, very solemnly. I understood, from that, that the Indian didn't know what blotting-paper was. It took me about half an hour to explain it to him, and in the end he said that he hadn't any in his store, but that if I liked he could order some for me from England. But by that time several of the thoughtful farmers, who were allowing their mules to rest, had heard what I was asking for. And they made remarks which were considered, in the Protectorate, to be funny.

One farmer said that Schalk Lourens was beginning to get very up-to-date, and that the next thing he would be ordering was a collar and tie.

"The last Boer who used blotting-paper," another man said, "was Piet Retief. When he signed that treaty with Dingaan."

They were still laughing in their meaningless way when I drove off, feeling very bitter at the thought that a nice girl like Lenie, who was so sensible in other respects, should have got me into that unpleasant situation.

On my way back over the border I had to pass the Bechuana school. And that was where, in the end, I obtained the blotting-paper. I got a few sheets from the kaffir schoolmaster. In exchange for the blotting-paper I gave him half a can of black axle-grease, which he explained that he wanted for rubbing on his hair. I did not think that he was a very highly-educated kaffir schoolmaster.

And when I took the blotting-paper back to Koedoesrand, I did not mention where I had obtained it. Consequently, I did not tell them, either, that the kaffir schoolmaster at Ramoutsa had made many enquiries of me in regard to a Baas Johnny de Clerk. There was no need for me to enlighten them. For I knew that the schoolmaster had told me only the truth, and that, therefore, it would all be found out in time.

In the weeks that followed I saw very little of Piet Venter and Lenie.

But I heard that Johnny de Clerk was still travelling about the neighbourhood, selling insurance. I also heard that he was in the habit of calling rather frequently at Piet Venter's house, to the annoyance of Gert Oosthuizen, the young farmer who was betrothed to Lenie.

And so the days passed by, as they do in the Marico, quietly.

Now and again vague stories reached me to the effect that Johnny de Clerk was seeing more and more of Lenie Venter, and that Gert Oosthuizen was viewing the matter with growing dissatisfaction. For these reasons I couldn't go to Koedoesrand. I realised that if I saw Piet Venter it would be my duty to tell him all I knew. And, somehow, there was something that prevented me.

The dry season passed and the rains came, and the dams were full. Then, one day, the whole Marico knew this thing about Johnny de Clerk. And, shortly afterwards, I went again to see Piet Venter at Koedoesrand.

But, in the meantime, Johnny de Clerk had had rather an unpleasant time. For, when they found out that, in his ignorant way, the kaffir schoolmaster was right to look upon the insurance agent as his son-in-law, a number of farmers waited until Johnny de Clerk again went to call on Lenie Venter. And they threw him into the dam, which was full with the rains, and when he came out his blue suit was very bedraggled, and his light hat was still in the water.

And so Johnny de Clerk left the Marico. But nobody could say for sure whether he went back to Pretoria, where he had come from, or to the Bechuana hut in Ramoutsa, where one of the farmers told him to go, when he kicked him.

The last time I saw Lenie Venter in her father's voorkamer was just before she married Gert Oosthuizen. And Gert was talking sentimental words to her, in a heavy fashion. But most of the time Lenie's face was turned away from Gert's, as she sat, with a far-off look in her dark eyes, drawing small circles on a piece of blotting-paper.

Brown Mamba

"GOD, that was terrible," Hendrik van Jaarsveld ejaculated, "and to think that it might have been me."

Then he cupped his hands and called. A few minutes later Piet Uys emerged from a clump of white thorn-bushes, carrying a Mauser.

"What's wrong, Hendrik?" Piet Uys asked. But there was no need for the other man to reply. There was that body lying beside the ox-wagon.

"Mamba?" Piet enquired.

"Brown mamba," Hendrik van Jaarsveld answered.

The two men took off their hats in silence. There was nothing to be done about it. For in the Marico District death and brown mamba are synonymous terms, and everybody knows that you can't do very much about death.

For a bite from a bakkop or a puff-adder or a ringhals, a sharp knife and permanganate of potash crystals are nearly always efficacious. But when a man is bitten by a mamba it is different. Then it is the Lord's will that a prayer should be said over his open grave, and that a hymn should be sung before the hole in the veld is covered up again with the red earth.

Hendrik van Jaarsveld and Piet Uys had trekked from Schweizer-Reneke because of the drought. With their wagons and cattle they had journeyed north through the Transvaal, coming to a halt at the foot of the Dwarsberge, where there was pasture.

They had been at this outspan for several weeks, with little to do besides shooting springbok in the vlaktes. But now they had to set about burying the kaffir herdsman.

The two white men stood by while the kaffirs dug the grave. Hendrik van Jaarsveld and two kaffirs then proceeded to wrap an old blanket round the body. They did their work awkwardly for, as undertakers, they were still amateurs. The herdsman had died with his left hand pressed under his right armpit, in an attempt to relieve the pain in his finger where the snake had bitten him.

When they moved him, the corpse's hand flapped stiffly on to his thigh. Hendrik turned his head away, but not before he had seen the grim mass into which the mamba's fangs had converted the dead man's hand.

"Yes, they say the hand is the worst place for a snakebite," Piet Uys remarked casually from where he stood, a few paces off. "The hand or the face. They say that if a mamba bites you in the hand you're dead before you strike the ground."

To Hendrik van Jaarsveld his companion's words sounded harsh and grating. He wished Piet would keep quiet. Like the kaffirs. They knew that death was a solemn thing. And the veld knew it, too. The veld was still – very still. Always the veld is still in the presence of death.

Suddenly Hendrik grew afraid. It was a vague fear he couldn't understand. But it made him feel very lonely. He seemed to be alone under the sky with the dead herdsman. The corpse and he seemed to be alone together. Piet and the kaffirs were apart from him somehow. He remembered having had that same feeling once before when he had shot a ribbok.

He had disembowelled the ribbok and was fastening two of its legs together so that he could carry it home across his shoulders. It was then that that strange feeling came to him, a feeling of intimacy and under-standing with the dead ribbok. Now, when he was standing over the herdsman and getting ready to lower him into the grave, that queer sense of companionship with the dead came to him again. It was fright-ening.

In the heat of the tropic noonday Hendrik shivered.

Piet Uys spoke again.

"Did you see the mamba?" he asked.

"Yes," Hendrik answered shortly.

"Did *he* see the mamba?" Piet asked again.

"No," Hendrik replied.

Hendrik had noticed that Piet refrained from mentioning the dead herdsman by name. Here was something inexplicable for you, Hendrik reflected. As soon as a man died you were afraid to go on talking of him by name. It was a singular thing.

"Yes, they say it is very often the case," Piet remarked. Hendrik started. But Piet's next words showed that he had not really broken in on Hendrik's thoughts. Still, it was disquieting.

"Yes," Piet went on, "they say that very often when you get bitten by a mamba, you die without having seen the snake. The mamba just glides out of the grass behind you and is gone again before you quite know what has happened. The whole thing is so sudden."

Hendrik did not answer. For some reason he did not want Piet to have the satisfaction of being told that his reconstruction of the incident was correct. Nevertheless, that was just how the thing had occurred. The herdsman was walking towards the wagon. He shouted something, not very loudly. And the next thing that Hendrik saw were brown coils vanishing into the grass with lightning movements, and the herdsman falling beside the wagon in a quivering heap. In his mind Hendrik could still see the glint of the sun on the sleek brown body of the snake.

"They also say – " Piet Uys began again.

But Hendrik interrupted him.

He did not like the callous way in which Piet spoke about those things. Just as though it were an ordinary matter for a man to die like this, of snakebite, before their eyes, without his having had time, even, to make his peace with God. "You are older than I, Oom Piet," Hendrik said. "Will you pray?" By that time the body had been lowered into the earth.

The white men stood together on one side of the grave. The kaffirs crowded together in a bunch on the other side. They were all bareheaded. Piet Uys did not pray long.

"Amen," Hendrik said when Piet had finished.

"Amen," the kaffirs said after him, self-conscious on account of their unfamiliarity with the white man's burial rites. They were Bechuanas, and had a different way of disposing of the dead.

"Anyway, he was a good kaffir," Piet Uys said, flinging a handful of earth into the grave, "we will sing a hymn for him, too. We will sing 'Rust Myn Ziel'."

Accordingly, the two white men sang a verse of this Dutch Reformed Church hymn, the kaffirs joining in as best they could.

Then the grave was covered up and the burial was over.

Hendrik van Jaarsveld was glad that the rainy season was approaching, bringing with it the prospect of the termination of the drought in Schweizer-Reneke. Then he could inspan his ox-wagon and trek home with his cattle. It was unnatural living alone like this in the bush with Piet Uys and the kaffirs. He wanted company.

It was very difficult having only one white man to talk to all the time, he decided. Especially when that man was Piet Uys. Piet said such stupid things, too. For instance, after the burial of the herdsman, he had said: "You know, Hendrik, they say that lightning never strikes in the same place twice. Well, it's the same with a mamba. It never strikes twice in the same place, either."

At this Piet had slapped Hendrik on the shoulder, expecting him to join in the joke – whatever it was.

"That's a good one, isn't it, Hendrik?" Piet said, "and I thought it out myself."

"I hope we're back in Schweizer-Reneke before you think out the next one," Hendrik answered; then, because Piet looked at him questioningly, he added quickly, "I mean, so that you will have more people to tell it to."

"I see," Piet answered, and turned away.

Since then their relations had been strained.

Piet had gone into the bush after game and Hendrik was glad to be alone. He sat on a fallen tree-trunk and gazed absently in the direction in which Piet had gone.

A rifle report rang out, echoing from krantz to krantz across the veld. Hendrik knew there would be no further shots. That was Piet Uys's way. He would go on patiently stalking a buck for hours on end, and he never fired until he was absolutely sure of his shot. It was Piet's boast that he always went with only one cartridge in his Mauser, and that he invariably brought back either a buck or the live cartridge.

From the distance of the report Hendrik worked it out that Piet would be back fairly soon. He didn't relish that very much. It was pleasant sitting alone in the sun, on a tree-trunk that had been hollowed out by the white ants.

Suddenly, as he pictured Piet bending over the buck, slashing away into the warm flesh with his hunting knife, Hendrik realised that he was again becoming subject to that sense of intimacy with dead things – the feeling that possessed him when he disembowelled the ribbok in the vlakte – the feeling that had come to him when he wrapped the dead herdsman in the blanket.

He was frightened.

He looked around. If only he could see a kaffir he would feel better. But he remembered that the kaffirs were all away with the cattle. He was shivering. The Marico was an unhealthy place to be in, he reflected. The sun and the stones and the thorn-trees. It was maddening. Nothing but thorn-trees and stones and the sun. It was a good country to come to once in a while. But you hadn't to stay long. And you must have company. You must have somebody with you who wasn't like Piet Uys.

He thought of Piet, walking through the bush, with a buck slung over his shoulder, every step bringing him nearer. Well, perhaps even Piet was better than this intense loneliness. He stared out into the bush. Piet wouldn't be long now.

But there was that buck that Piet would be carrying. Hendrik decided that he might even try to talk to Piet about this queer feeling that overtook him now and then. It was just possible that Piet might understand. He might even have had similar queer emotions about things.

Yes, when Piet came, he would talk to him about it.

Shortly afterwards Piet came. Hendrik saw him through the trees. He took off his hat and waved. Piet waved back. Suddenly Hendrik felt, darting through his left hand, a monstrous pain. He saw Piet fling down his rifle and the buck and come running up towards him. Then Hendrik slipped from the tree-trunk and, with his hand pressed tight under his armpit, rolled over and over in the grass.

He came to rest with his legs on an ant-hill and his head in a slight depression. It was a funny sort of way to lie, Hendrik thought. But what seemed stranger still, was that the pain, which for a while had swept through and through his whole body, had left him. He remembered thrusting his hand into his armpit. He would remove it and find out what caused the pain.

But he couldn't move his hand. That was queer. He wanted to sit up. He couldn't do that either.

"Piet," he tried to call. But his lips remained motionless, and no sound came.

That was funny, Hendrik thought.

Then when Piet Uys approached and took off his hat very slowly, Hendrik van Jaarsveld understood.

"God, how terrible," Piet Uys said, "and how easily it might have been me."

Dream by the Bluegums

N the heat of the midday – Oom Schalk Lourens said – Adriaan Naudé and I were glad to be resting there, shaded by the tall bluegums that stood in a clump by the side of the road.

I sat on the grass, with my head and shoulders supported against a large stone. Adriaan Naudé, who had begun by leaning against a tree-trunk with his legs crossed and his fingers interlaced behind his head and his elbows out, lowered himself to the ground by degrees; for a short while he remained seated on his haunches; then he sighed and slid forward, very carefully, until he was lying stretched out at full length, with his face in the grass.

And all this while Adriaan Naudé was murmuring about how lazy kaffirs are, and about the fact that the kaffir Jonas should already have returned with the mule-cart, and about how, if you wanted a job done properly, you had to do it yourself. I agreed with Adriaan Naudé that Jonas had been away rather long with the mule-cart; he ought to be back quite soon, now, I said.

"The curse of the Transvaal," Adriaan Naudé explained, stretching himself out further along the grass, and yawning, "the curse of the Transvaal is the indolence of the kaffirs."

"Yes, Neef Adriaan," I replied. "You are quite correct. It would perhaps have been better if one of us had gone along in the mule-cart with Jonas."

"It's not so bad for you, Neef Schalk," Adriaan Naudé went on, yawning again. "You have got a big comfortable stone to rest your head and shoulders against. Whereas I have got to lie flat down on the dry grass with all the sharp points sticking into me. You are always like that, Neef Schalk. You always pick the best for yourself."

By the unreasonable nature of his remarks I could tell that Adriaan Naudé was being overtaken by a spell of drowsiness.

"You are always like that," Adriaan went on. "It's one of the low traits of your character. Always picking the best for yourself. There was that time in Zeerust, for instance. People always mention that – when they want to talk about how low a man can be. . . "

I could see that the heat of the day and his condition of being half-asleep might lead Adriaan Naudé to say things that he would no doubt be sorry for afterwards. So I interrupted him, speaking very earnestly for his own good.

"It's quite true, Neef Adriaan," I said, "that this stone against which I am lying is the only one in the vicinity. But I can't help that any more than I can help this clump of bluegums being here. It's funny about these bluegums, now, growing like this by the side of the road, when the rest of the veld around here is bare. I wonder who planted them. As for this stone, Neef Adriaan, it is not my fault that I saw it first. It was just luck. But you can knock out your pipe against it whenever you want to."

This offer seemed to satisfy Adriaan. At all events, he didn't pursue the argument. I noticed that his breathing had become very slow and deep and regular; and the last remark that he made was so muffled as to be almost unintelligible. It was: "To think that a white man can fall so low."

From that I judged that Adriaan Naudé was dreaming about something.

It was very pleasant, there, on the yellow grass, by the roadside, underneath the bluegums, whose shadows slowly lengthened as midday passed into afternoon. Nowhere was there sound or movement. The whole world was at rest, with the silence of the dust on the deserted road, with the peace of the bluegums' shadows. My companion's measured breathing seemed to come from very far away.

Then it was that a strange thing happened.

What is in the first place remarkable about the circumstance that I am now going to relate to you is that it shows you clearly how short a dream is. And how much you can dream in just a few moments. In the second place, as you'll see when I get to the end of it, this story proves how right in broad daylight a queer thing can take place – almost in front of your eyes, as it were – and you may wonder about it for ever afterwards, and you will never understand it.

Well, as I was saying, what with Adriaan Naudé lying asleep within a few feet of me, and everything being so still, I was on the point of also dropping off to sleep, when, in the distance – so small that I could barely distinguish its outlines – I caught sight of the mule-cart whose return Adriaan and I were awaiting. From where I lay, with my head on the stone, I had a clear view of the road all the way up to where it disappeared over the bult.

For a while I lay watching the approach of the mule-cart. As I have said, it was still very far away. But gradually it drew nearer and I made out more of the details. The dark forms of the mules. The shadowy figure of Jonas, the driver.

But as I gazed I felt my eyelids getting heavy. I told myself that with the glare of the sun on the road I would not be able to keep my eyes open much longer. I remember thinking how foolish it would be to fall asleep, then, with the mule-cart only a short distance away. It would pull up almost immediately, and I would have to wake up again. I told myself I was being foolish – and, of course, I fell asleep.

It was while I was still telling myself that in a few moments the mule-cart would be coming to a stop in the shadow of the bluegums that my eyes closed and I fell asleep. And I started to dream. And from this you can tell how swift a thing a dream is, and how much you can dream in a few moments.

For I know the exact moment in which I started to dream. It was when I was looking very intently at the driver of the mule-cart and I suddenly saw, to my amazement, that the driver was no longer Jonas, the kaffir, but Adriaan Naudé. And seated beside Adriaan Naudé was a girl in a white frock. She had yellow hair that hung far down over her shoulders and her name was Francina. The next minute the mule-cart drew up and Jonas jumped off and tied the reins to a wheel.

So it was in between those flying moments that I dreamt about Adriaan Naudé and Francina.

"It is difficult to believe, Francina," Adriaan Naudé was saying, nodding his head in my direction, "it is difficult to believe that a white man can sink so low. If I tell you what happened in Zeerust – "

I was getting annoyed, now. After all, Francina was a complete stranger, and Adriaan had no right to slander me in that fashion. What was more, I had a very simple explanation of the Zeerust incident. I felt that if only I could be alone with Francina for a few minutes I would be able to convince her that what had happened in Zeerust was not to my discredit at all.

Furthermore, I would be able to tell her one or two things about Adriaan; things of so unfortunate a character that even if she believed about the Zeerust affair it would not matter much. Because, compared with Adriaan Naudé, the most inferior kind of man would still look as noble and heroic as Wolraad Woltemade that you read about in the school books.

But even as I started to talk to Francina I realised that there was no

89

need for me to say anything. She put her hand on my arm and looked at me; and the sun was on her hair and the shadows of the bluegums were in her eyes; and by the way she smiled at me I knew that nothing Adriaan could say about me would ever make any difference to her.

Moreover, Adriaan Naudé had gone. You know how it is in a dream. He had completely disappeared, leaving Francina and me alone by the roadside. And I knew that Adriaan Naudé would not trouble us any more. All he had come there for was to bring Francina along to me. Yet I regretted his departure, somehow. It seemed too easy, almost. There were a couple of things about Adriaan Naudé that I felt Francina really ought to know.

Then it all changed, suddenly. I seemed to know that it was only a dream and that I wasn't really standing up under the trees with Francina. I seemed to know that I was actually resting on the grass, with my head and shoulders resting against a stone. I even heard the mule-cart jolting over the rough part of the road.

But in the next instant I was dreaming again.

I dreamt that Francina was explaining to me, in gentle and sorrowful tones, that she couldn't stay any longer; and that she had put her hand on my arm for the last time, in farewell; she said I was not to follow her, but that I had to close my eyes when she turned away; for no one was to know where she had come from.

While she was saying these things my eyes lighted on her frock, which was brilliant in the sunshine. But it seemed an old-fashioned sort of frock; the kind that was worn many years before. Then, in the same moment, I saw her face, and it seemed to me that her smile was old-fashioned, somehow. It was a sweet smile, and her face, turned upwards, was strangely beautiful; but I felt in some queer way that women had smiled like that very long ago.

It was a vivid dream. Part of it seemed more real than life; as is frequently the case with a dream on the veld, fleetingly, in the heat of the noonday.

I asked Francina where she lived.

"Not far from here," she answered, "no, not far. But you may not follow me. None may go back with me."

She still smiled, in that way in which women smiled long ago; but as she spoke there came into her eyes a look of such intense sorrow that

I was afraid to ask why I could not accompany her. And when she told me to close my eyes I had no power to protest.

And, of course, I didn't close my eyes. Instead, I opened them. Just as Jonas was jumping down from the mule-cart to fasten the reins on to a wheel.

Adriaan Naudé woke up about the same time that I did, and asked Jonas why he had been away so long, and spoke more about the indolence of the kaffirs. And I got up from the grass and stretched my limbs and wondered about dreams. It seemed incredible that I could have dreamt so much in such a few moments.

And there was a strange sadness in my heart because the dream had gone. My mind was filled with a deep sense of loss. I told myself that it was foolish to have feelings like that about a dream: even though it was a particularly vivid dream, and part of it seemed more real than life.

Then, when we were ready to go, Adriaan Naudé took out his pipe; before filling it he stooped down as though to knock the ash out of it, as I had invited him to do before we fell asleep. But it so happened that Adriaan Naudé did not ever knock his pipe out against that stone.

"That's funny," I heard Adriaan say as he bent forward.

I saw what he was about; so I knelt down and helped him. When we had cleared away the accumulation of yellow grass and dead leaves at the foot of the stone we found that the inscription on it, though battered, was quite legible. It was very simply worded. Just a date chiselled on to the stone. And below the date a name: Francina Malherbe.

The Gramophone

THAT was a terrible thing that happened with Krisjan Lemmer, Oom Schalk Lourens said. It was pretty bad for me, of course, but it was much worse for Krisjan.

I remember well when it happened, for that was the time when the first gramophone came into the Marico Bushveld. Krisjan bought the machine off a Jew trader from Pretoria. It's funny when you come to think of it. When there is anything that we Boers don't want you can be quite sure that the Jew traders will bring it to us, and that we'll buy it, too.

I remember how I laughed when a Jew came to my house once with a hollow piece of glass that had a lot of silver stuff in it. The Jew told me that the silver in the glass moved up and down to show you if it was hot or cold. Of course, I said that was all nonsense. I know when it is cold enough for me to put on my woollen shirt and jacket, without having first to go and look at that piece of glass. And I also know when it is too hot to work – which it is almost all the year round in this part of the Marico Bushveld. In the end I bought the thing. But it has never been the same since little Annie stirred her coffee with it.

Anyway, if the Jew traders could bring us the miltsiek, we would buy that off them as well, and pay them so much down, and the rest when all our cattle are dead.

Therefore, when a trader brought Krisjan Lemmer a second-hand gramophone, Krisjan sold some sheep and bought the thing. For many miles round the people came to hear the machine talk. Krisjan was very proud of his gramophone, and when he turned the handle and put in the little sharp pins, it was just like a child that has found something new to play with. The people who came to hear the gramophone said that it was very wonderful what things man would think of making when once the devil had taken a hold on him properly. They said that, if nothing else, the devil has got good brains. I also thought it was wonderful, not that the gramophone could talk, but that people wanted to listen to it doing something that a child of seven could do as well. Most of the songs the gramophone played were in English. But there was one song in Afrikaans. It was "O Brandewyn laat my staan." Krisjan played that often; the man on the round plate sang it rather well. Only the way he pronounced the words made it seem as though he was a German trying to make "O Brandewyn laat my staan" sound English. It was just like the rooineks, I thought. First they took our country and governed it for us in a better way than we could do ourselves; now they wanted to make improvements in our language for us.

But if people spoke much about Krisjan Lemmer's gramophone, they spoke a great deal more about the unhappy way in which he and his wife lived together. Krisjan Lemmer was then about thirty-five. He was a big, strongly-built man, and when he moved about you could see the muscles of his shoulders stand out under his shirt. He was also a surprisingly good-natured man who seldom became annoyed about anything. Even with the big drought, when he had to pump water for his cattle all day and the pump broke, so that he could get no water for his cattle, he just walked into the house and lit his pipe and said that it was the Lord's will. He said that perhaps it was as well that the pump broke, because, if the Lord wanted the cattle to get water, He wouldn't have sent the drought. That was the kind of man Krisjan Lemmer was. And he would never have set hand to the pump again, either, was it not that the next day rain fell, whereby Krisjan knew that the Lord meant him to understand that the drought was over. Yet, when anything angered him he was bad.

But the unfortunate part of Krisjan Lemmer was that he could not get on with his wife Susannah. Always they quarrelled. Susannah, as we knew, was a good deal younger than her husband, but often she didn't look so very much younger. She was small and fair. Her skin had not been much darkened by the Bushveld sun, for she always wore a very wide kappie, the folds of which she pinned down over the upper part of her face whenever she went out of the house. Her hair was the colour of the beard you see on the yellow mealies just after they have ripened. She had very quiet ways. In company she hardly ever talked, unless it was to say that the Indian shopkeeper in Ramoutsa put roasted kremetart roots with the coffee he sold us, or that the spokes of the mule-cart came loose if you didn't pour water over them.

You see, what she said were things that everybody knew and that no one argued about. Even the Indian storekeeper didn't argue about the kremetart roots. He knew that was the best part of his coffee. And yet, although she was so quiet and unassuming, Susannah was always quarrelling with her husband. This, of course, was foolish of her, especially as Krisjan was a man with gentle ways until somebody purposely annoyed him. Then he was not quite so gentle. For instance, there was the time when the chief of the Mtosa kaffirs passed him in the veld and said "Good morning" without taking the leopard skin off his head and calling Krisjan baas. Krisjan was fined ten pounds by the magistrate and had to pay for the doctor during the three months that the Mtosa chief walked with a stick.

One day I went to Krisjan Lemmer's farm to borrow a roll of baling-wire for the teff. Krisjan had just left for the krantz to see if he could shoot a ribbok. Susannah was at home alone. I could see that she had been crying. So I went and sat next to her on the riempies-bank and took her hand.

"Don't cry, Susannah," I said, "everything will be all right. You must just learn to understand Krisjan a little better. He is not a bad fellow in his way."

At first she was angry with me for saying anything against Krisjan, and she told me to go home. But afterwards she became more reasonable about it, allowing me to move up a bit closer to her and to hold her hand a little tighter. In that way I comforted her. I would have comforted her even more, perhaps, only I couldn't be sure how long Krisjan would remain in the krantz; and I didn't like what happened to the Mtosa kaffir chief.

I asked her to play the gramophone for me, not because I wanted to hear it, but because you always pretend to take an interest in the things that your friends like, especially when you borrow a roll of baling-wire off them. When anybody visits me and gets my youngest son Willie to recite texts from the Bible, I know that before he leaves he is going to ask me if I will be using my mealie-planter this week.

So Susannah put the round plate on the thing, and turned the handle, and the gramophone played "O Brandewyn laat my staan." You couldn't hear too well what the man was singing, but I have said all that before.

Susannah laughed as she listened, and in that moment somehow she seemed very much younger than her husband. She looked very pretty, too. But I noticed also that when the music ended it was as though she was crying.

Then Krisjan came in. I left shortly afterwards. But I had heard his footsteps coming up the path, so there was no need for me to leave in a hurry.

94

But just before I went Susannah brought in coffee. It was weak coffee; but I didn't say anything about it. I am very much like an Englishman that way. It's what they call manners. When I am visiting strangers and they give me bad coffee I don't throw it out and say that the stuff isn't fit for a kaffir. I just drink it and then don't go back to that house again. But Krisjan spoke about it.

"Vrou," he said, "the coffee is weak."

"Yes," Susannah answered.

"It's very weak," he went on.

"Yes," she replied.

"Why do you always. . . " Krisjan began again.

"Oh, go to hell," Susannah said.

Then they went at it, swearing at one another, and they didn't even hear me when, on leaving, in the manner of the Bushveld, I said, "Goodbye and may the good Lord bless us all."

It was a dark night that time, about three months later, when I again went to Krisjan Lemmer's house by mule-cart. I was leaving early in the morning for Zeerust with a load of mealies and wanted to borrow Krisjan's wagon-sail. Before I was halfway to his house it started raining. Big drops fell on my face. There was something queer about the sound of the wind in the wet trees, and when I drove through the poort where the Government Road skirts the line of the Dwarsberge the place looked very dark to me. I thought of death and things like that. I thought of pale strange ghosts that come upon you from behind. . . suddenly. I felt sorry, then, that I had not brought a kaffir along. It was not that I was afraid of being alone; but it would have been useful, on the return, to have a kaffir sitting in the back of the mule-cart to look after the wagon-sail for me.

The rain stopped.

I came to the farm's graveyard, where had been buried members of the Lemmer family and of other families who had lived there before the Lemmers, and I knew that I was near the house. It seemed to me to be a very silly sort of thing to make a graveyard so close to the road. There's no sense in that. Some people, for instance, who are ignorant and a bit superstitious are liable, perhaps, to start shivering a little, especially if the night is dark and there is a wind and the mule-cart is bumpy.

There were no lights in the Lemmers' house when I got there. I

95

knocked a long time before the door was opened, and then it was Krisjan Lemmer standing in the doorway with a lantern held above his head. He looked agitated at first, until he saw who it was and then he smiled.

"Come in, Neef Schalk," he said. "I am pleased you are here. I was beginning to feel lonely – you know, the rain and the wind and – "

"But you are not alone," I replied. "What about Susannah?"

"Oh, Susannah has gone back to her mother," Krisjan answered. "She went yesterday."

We went into the voorkamer and sat down. Krisjan Lemmer lit a candle and we talked and smoked. The window-panes looked black against the night. The wind blew noisily through openings between the wall and the thatched roof. The candle-flame flickered unsteadily. It could not be pleasant for Krisjan Lemmer alone in that house without his wife. He looked restless and uncomfortable. I tried to make a joke about it.

"What's the matter with you, Krisjan?" I asked. "You're looking so unhappy, anybody would think you've still got your wife here with you."

Krisjan laughed, and I wished he hadn't. His laughter did not sound natural; it was too loud. Somehow I got a cold kind of feeling in my blood. It was rather a frightening thing, the wind blowing incessantly outside the house, and inside the house a man laughing too loudly.

"Let us play the gramophone, Krisjan," I said.

By that time I knew how to work the thing myself. So I put in one of the little pins and started it off. But before doing that I had taken the gramophone off its table and placed it on the floor in front of my chair, where I could get at it more easily.

It seemed different without Susannah's being there. Also, it looked peculiar to me that she should leave so suddenly. And there was no doubt about it that Krisjan was acting in a strange way that I didn't like. He was restless. When he lit his pipe he had to strike quite a number of matches. And all that time round the house the wind blew very loudly.

The gramophone began to play.

The plate was "O Brandewyn laat my staan."

I thought of Susannah and of the way she had listened three months before to that same song. I glanced up quickly at Krisjan, and as soon as he caught my eye he looked away. I was glad when the gramophone finished playing. And there was something about Krisjan that made me feel that he was pleased also. He seemed very queer about Susannah.

Then an awful thought occurred to me.

You know sometimes you get a thought like that and you know that it is true.

I got up unsteadily and took my hat. I saw that all round the place where the gramophone stood the dung floor of the voorkamer had been loosened and then stamped down again. The candle threw flickering shadows over the floor and over the clods of loose earth that had not been stamped down properly.

I drove back without the bucksail.

The Prophet

NO, I never came across the Prophet van Rensburg, the man who told General Kemp that it was the right time to rebel against the English. As you know, General Kemp followed his advice and they say that General Kemp still believed in Van Rensburg's prophecies, even after the two of them were locked up in the Pretoria Gaol.

But I knew another prophet. His name was Erasmus. Stephanus Erasmus. Van Rensburg could only foretell that so and so was going to happen, and then he was wrong, sometimes. But with Stephanus Erasmus it was different. Erasmus used to make things come true just by prophesying them.

You can see what that means. And yet, in the end I wondered about Stephanus Erasmus.

There are lots of people like Van Rensburg who can just foretell the future, but when a man comes along who can actually make the future, then you feel that you can't make jokes about him. All the farmers in Droëdal talked about Stephanus Erasmus with respect. Even when he wasn't present to hear what was being said about him. Because there would always be somebody to go along and tell him if you happened to make some slighting remark about him.

I know, because once in Piet Fourie's house I said that if I was a great prophet like Stephanus Erasmus I would try and prophesy myself a new pair of veldskoens, seeing that his were all broken on top and you could see two corns and part of an ingrowing toenail. After that things went all wrong on my farm for six months. So I knew that Piet Fourie had told the prophet what I had said. Amongst other things six of my best trek-oxen died of the miltsiekte.

After that, whenever I wanted to think anything unflattering about Stephanus Erasmus I went right out into the veld and did it all there. You can imagine that round that time I went into the veld alone very often. It wasn't easy to forget about the six trek-oxen.

More than once I hoped that Stephanus Erasmus would also take it into his head to tell General Kemp that it was the right time to go into rebellion. But Erasmus was too wise for that. I remember once when we were all together just before a meeting of the Dwarsberg School Committee I asked Stephanus about this.

"What do you think of this new wheel-tax, Oom Stephanus?" I said. "Don't you think the people should go along with their rifles and hoist the Vierkleur over the magistrates' court at Zeerust?"

Erasmus looked at me and I lowered my eyes. I felt sorry in a way that I had spoken. His eyes seemed to look right through me. I felt that to him I looked like a springbok that has been shot and cut open, and you can see his heart and his ribs and his liver and his stomach and all the rest of his insides. It was not very pleasant to be sitting talking to a man who regards you as nothing more than a cut-open springbok.

But Stephanus Erasmus went on looking at me. I became frightened. If he had said to me then, "You know you are just a cut-open spring-bok," I would have said, "Yes, Oom Stephanus, I know." I could see then that he had a great power. He was just an ordinary sort of farmer on the outside, with a black beard and dark eyes and a pair of old shoes that were broken on top. But inside he was terrible. I began to be afraid for my remaining trek-oxen.

Then he spoke, slowly and with wisdom.

"There are also magistrates' courts at Mafeking and Zwartruggens and Rysmierbult," he said. "In fact there is a magistrates' court in every town I have been in along the railway line. And all these magistrates' courts collect wheel-tax," Oom Stephanus said.

I could see then that he not only had great power inside him, but that he was also very cunning. He never went in for any wild guessing, like saying to a stranger, "You are a married man with five children and in your inside jacket-pocket is a letter from the Kerkraad asking you to become an ouderling." I have seen some so-called fortune-tellers say that to a man they had never seen in their lives before in the hope that they might be right.

You know, it is a wonderful thing this, about being a prophet. I have thought much about it, and what I know about it I can't explain. But I know it has got something to do with death. This is one of the things I have learnt in the Marico, and I don't think you could learn it anywhere else. It is only when you have had a great deal of time in which to do nothing but think and look at the veld and at the sky where there have been no rain-clouds for many months, that you grow to an understand-ing of these things.

Then you know that being a prophet and having power is very simple. But it is also something very terrible. And you know then that there are men and women who are unearthly, and it is this that makes them greater than kings. For a king can lose his power when people take it away from him, but a prophet can never lose his power – if he is a real prophet.

It was the schoolchildren who first began talking about this. I have noticed how often things like this start with the stories of kaffirs and children.

Anyway, a very old kaffir had come to live at the outspan on the road to Ramoutsa. Nobody knew where he had come from, except that when questioned he would lift up his arm very slowly and point towards the west. There is nothing in the west. There is only the Kalahari Desert. And from his looks you could easily believe that this old kaffir had lived in the desert all his life. There was something about his withered body that reminded you of the Great Drought.

We found out that this kaffir's name was Mosiko. He had made himself a rough shelter of thorn-bushes and old mealie bags. And there he lived alone. The kaffirs round about brought him mealies and beer, and from what they told us it appeared that he was not very grateful for these gifts, and when the beer was weak he swore vilely at the persons who brought it.

As I have said, it was the kaffirs who first took notice of him. They said he was a great witch-doctor. But later on white people also started taking him presents. And they asked him questions about what was going to happen. Sometimes Mosiko told them what they wanted to know. At other times he was impudent and told them to go and ask Baas Stephanus Erasmus.

You can imagine what a stir this created.

"Yes," Frans Steyn said to us one afternoon, "and when I asked this kaffir whether my daughter Anna should get married to Gert right away or whether she should go to High School to learn English, Mosiko said that I had to ask Baas Stephanus. 'Ask him,' he said, 'that one is too easy for me'."

Then the people said that this Mosiko was an impertinent kaffir, and that the only thing Stephanus could do was not to take any notice of him.

I watched closely to see what Erasmus was going to do about it. I could see that the kaffir's impudence was making him mad. And when people said to him, "Do not take any notice of Mosiko, Oom Stephanus, he is a lazy old kaffir," anyone could see that this annoyed him more than anything else. He suspected that they said this out of politeness. And there is nothing that angers you more than when those who used to fear you start being polite to you.

The upshot of the business was that Stephanus Erasmus went to the outspan where Mosiko lived. He said he was going to boot him back into the Kalahari, where he came from. Now, it was a mistake for Stephanus to have gone out to see Mosiko. For Mosiko looked really important to have the prophet coming to visit him. The right thing always is for the servant to visit the master.

All of us went along with Stephanus.

On the way down he said, "I'll kick him all the way out of Zeerust. It is bad enough when kaffirs wear collars and ties in Johannesburg and walk on the pavements reading newspapers. But we can't allow this sort of thing in the Marico."

But I could see that for some reason Stephanus was growing angry as we tried to pretend that we were determined to have Mosiko shown up. And this was not the truth. It was only Erasmus's quarrel. It was not our affair at all.

We got to the outspan.

Mosiko had hardly any clothes on. He sat up against a bush with his back bent and his head forward near his knees. He had many wrinkles. Hundreds of them. He looked to be the oldest man in the world. And yet there was a kind of strength about the curve of his back and I knew the meaning of it. It seemed to me that with his back curved in that way, and the sun shining on him and his head bent forward, Mosiko could be much greater and do more things just by sitting down than other men could do by working hard and using cunning. I felt that Mosiko could sit down and do nothing and yet be more powerful than the Kommandant-General.

He seemed to have nothing but what the sun and the sand and the grass had given him, and yet that was more than what all the men in the world could give him.

I was glad that I was there that day, at the meeting of the wizards.

Stephanus Erasmus knew who Mosiko was, of course. But I wasn't sure if Mosiko knew Stephanus. So I introduced them. On another day people would have laughed at the way I did it. But at that moment it didn't seem so funny, somehow.

"Mosiko," I said, "this is Baas Prophet Stephanus Erasmus."

"And, Oom Stephanus," I said, "this is Witch-doctor Mosiko."

Mosiko raised his eyes slightly and glanced at Erasmus. Erasmus looked straight back at Mosiko and tried to stare him out of countenance. I knew the power with which Stephanus Erasmus could look at you. So I wondered what was going to happen. But Mosiko looked down again, and kept his eyes down on the sand.

Now, I remembered how I felt that day when Stephanus Erasmus had looked at me and I was ready to believe that I was a cut-open springbok. So I was not surprised at Mosiko's turning away his eyes. But in the same moment I realised that Mosiko looked down in the way that seemed to mean that he didn't think that Stephanus was a man of enough importance for him to want to stare out of countenance. It was as though he thought there were other things for him to do but look at Stephanus.

Then Mosiko spoke.

"Tell me what you want to know, Baas Stephanus," he said, "and I'll prophesy for you."

I saw the grass and the veld and the stones. I saw a long splash of sunlight on Mosiko's naked back. But for a little while I neither saw nor heard anything else. For it was a deadly thing that the kaffir had said to the white man. And I knew that the others also felt it was a deadly thing. We stood there, waiting. I was not sure whether to be glad or sorry that I had come. The time seemed so very long in passing.

"Kaffir," Stephanus said at last, "you have no right to be here on a white man's outspan. We have come to throw you off it. I am going to kick you, kaffir. Right now I am going to kick you. You'll see what a white man's boot is like."

Mosiko did not move. It did not seem as though he had heard anything Stephanus had said to him. He appeared to be thinking of something else – something very old and very far away.

Then Stephanus took a step forward. He paused for a moment. We all looked down.

Frans Steyn was the first to laugh. It was strange and unnatural at first to hear Frans Steyn's laughter. Everything up till then had been so tense and even frightening. But immediately afterwards we all burst out laughing together. We laughed loudly and uproariously. You could have heard us right at the other side of the bult.

I have told you about Stephanus Erasmus's veldskoens, and that they were broken on top. Well, now, in walking to the outspan, the last riem had burst loose, and Stephanus Erasmus stood there with his right foot raised from the ground and a broken shoe dangling from his instep.

Stephanus never kicked Mosiko. When we had finished laughing we got him to come back home. Stephanus walked slowly, carrying the broken shoe in his hand and picking the soft places to walk on, where the burnt grass wouldn't stick into his bare foot.

Stephanus Erasmus had lost his power.

But I knew that even if his shoe hadn't broken, Stephanus would never have kicked Mosiko. I could see by that look in his eyes that, when he took the step forward and Mosiko didn't move, Stephanus had been beaten for always.

Drieka and the Moon

THERE is a queer witchery about the moon when it is full – Oom Schalk Lourens remarked – especially the moon that hangs over the valley of the Dwarsberge in the summer time. It does strange things to your mind, the Marico moon, and in your heart are wild and fragrant fancies, and your thoughts go very far away. Then, if you have been sitting on your front stoep, thinking these thoughts, you sigh and murmur something about the way of the world, and carry your chair inside.

I have seen the moon in other places besides the Marico. But it is not the same, there.

Braam Venter, the man who fell off the Government lorry once, near Nietverdiend, says that the Marico moon is like a woman laying green flowers on a grave. Braam Venter often says things like that. Particularly since the time he fell off the lorry. He fell on his head, they say.

Always when the moon shines full like that it does something to our hearts that we wonder very much about and that we never understand. Always it awakens memories. And it is singular how different these memories are with each one of us.

Johannes Oberholzer says that the full moon always reminds him of one occasion when he was smuggling cattle over the Bechuanaland border. He says he never sees a full moon without thinking of the way it shone on the steel wire-cutters that he was holding in his hand when two mounted policemen rode up to him. And the next night Johannes Oberholzer again had a good view of the full moon; he saw it through the window of the place he was in. He says the moon was very large and very yellow, except for the black stripes in front of it.

And it was in the light of the full moon that hung over the thorn-trees that I saw Drieka Breytenbach.

Drieka was tall and slender. She had fair hair and blue eyes, and lots of people considered that she was the prettiest woman in the Marico. I thought so, too, that night I met her under the full moon by the thorn-trees. She had not been in the Bushveld very long. Her husband, Petrus Breytenbach, had met her and married her in the Schweizer-Reneke

District, where he had trekked with his cattle for a while during the big drought.

Afterwards, when Petrus Breytenbach was shot dead with his own Mauser by a kaffir working on his farm, Drieka went back to Schweizer-Reneke, leaving the Marico as strangely and as silently as she had come to it.

And it seemed to me that the Marico was a different place because Drieka Breytenbach had gone. And I thought of the moon, and the tricks it plays with your senses, and the stormy witchery that it flings at your soul. And I remembered what Braam Venter said, that the full moon is like a woman laying green flowers on a grave. And it seemed to me that Braam Venter's words were not so much nonsense, after all, and that worse things could happen to a man than that he should fall off a lorry on his head. And I thought of other matters.

But all this happened only afterwards.

When I saw Drieka that night she was leaning against a thorn-tree beside the road where it goes down to the drift. But I didn't recognise her at first. All I saw was a figure dressed in white with long hair hanging down loose over its shoulders. It seemed very unusual that a figure should be there like that at such a time of night. I remembered certain stories I had heard about white ghosts. I also remembered that a few miles back I had seen a boulder lying in the middle of the road. It was a fair-sized boulder and it might be dangerous for passing mule-carts. So I decided to turn back at once and move it out of the way.

I decided very quickly about the boulder. And I made up my mind so firmly that the saddle-girth broke from the sudden way in which I jerked my horse back on his haunches. Then the figure came forward and spoke, and I saw it was Drieka Breytenbach.

"Good evening," I said in answer to her greeting, "I was just going back because I had remembered about something."

"About ghosts?" she asked.

"No," I replied truthfully, "about a stone in the road."

Drieka laughed at that. So I laughed, too. And then Drieka laughed again. And then I laughed. In fact, we did quite a lot of laughing between us. I got off my horse and stood beside Drieka in the moonlight. And if somebody had come along at that moment and said that the predikant's mule-cart had been capsized by the boulder in the road I would have laughed still more.

That is the sort of thing the moon in the Marico does to you when it is full.

I didn't think of asking Drieka how she came to be there, or why her hair was hanging down loose, or who it was that she had been waiting for under the thorn-tree. It was enough that the moon was there, big and yellow across the veld, and that the wind blew softly through the trees and across the grass and against Drieka's white dress and against the mad singing of the stars.

Before I knew what was happening we were seated on the grass under the thorn-tree whose branches leant over the road. And I remember that for quite a while we remained there without talking, sitting side by side on the grass with our feet in the soft sand. And Drieka smiled at me with a misty sort of look in her eyes, and I saw that she was lovely.

I felt that it was not enough that we should go on sitting there in silence. I knew that a woman – even a moon-woman like Drieka – expected a man to be more than just good-humoured and honest. I knew that a woman wanted a man also to be an entertaining companion for her. So I beguiled the passing moments for Drieka with interesting conversation.

I explained to her how a few days before a pebble had worked itself into my veldskoen and had rubbed some skin off the top of one of my toes. I took off my veldskoen and showed her the place. I also told her about the rinderpest and about the way two of my cows had died of the miltsiek. I also knew a lot about blue-tongue in sheep, and about gallamsiekte and the haarwurm, and I talked to her airily about these things, just as easily as I am talking to you.

But, of course, it was the moonlight that did it. I never knew before that I was so good in this idle, butterfly kind of talk. And the whole thing was so innocent, too. I felt that if Drieka Breytenbach's husband, Petrus, were to come along and find us sitting there side by side, he would not be able to say much about it. At least, not very much.

After a while I stopped talking.

Drieka put her hand in mine.

"Oh, Schalk," she whispered, and the moon and that misty look were in her blue eyes. "Do tell me some more."

I shook my head.

"I am sorry, Drieka," I answered, "I don't know any more."

"But you must, Schalk," she said softly. "Talk to me about – about other things."

I thought steadily for some moments.

"Yes, Drieka," I said at length, "I have remembered something. There is one more thing I haven't told you about the blue-tongue in sheep – "

"No, no, not that," she interrupted, "talk to me about other things. About the moon, say."

So I told her two things that Braam Venter had said about the moon. I told her the green flower one and the other one.

"Braam Venter knows lots more things like that about the moon," I explained, "you'll see him next time you go to Zeerust for the Nagmaal. He is a short fellow with a bump on his head from where he fell – "

"Oh, no, Schalk," Drieka said again, shaking her head, so that a wisp of her fair hair brushed against my face, "I don't want to know about Braam Venter. Only about you. You think out something on your own about the moon and tell it to me."

I understood what she meant.

"Well, Drieka," I said thoughtfully. "The moon – the moon is all right."

"Oh, Schalk," Drieka cried. "That's much finer than anything Braam Venter could ever say – even with that bump on his head."

Of course, I told her that it was nothing and that I could perhaps say something even better if I tried. But I was very proud, all the same. And somehow it seemed that my words brought us close together. I felt that that handful of words, spoken under the full moon, had made a new and witch thing come into the life of Drieka and me.

We were holding hands then, sitting on the grass with our feet in the road, and Drieka leant her head on my shoulder, and her long hair stirred softly against my face, but I looked only at her feet. And I thought for a moment that I loved her. And I did not love her because her body was beautiful, or because she had red lips, or because her eyes were blue. In that moment I did not understand about her body or her lips or her eyes. I loved her for her feet; and because her feet were in the road next to mine.

And yet all the time I felt, far away at the back of my mind, that it was the moon that was doing these things to me.

"You have got good feet for walking on," I said to Drieka.

"Braam Venter would have said that I have got good feet for dancing on," Drieka answered, laughing. And I began to grow jealous of Braam Venter.

The next thing I knew was that Drieka had thrown herself into my arms.

"Do you think I am very beautiful, Schalk?" Drieka asked.

"You are very beautiful, Drieka," I answered slowly, "very beautiful."

"Will you do something for me, Schalk?" Drieka asked again, and her red lips were very close to my cheek. "Will you do something for me if I love you very much?"

"What do you want me to do, Drieka?"

She drew my head down to her lips and whispered hot words in my ear.

And so it came about that I thrust her from me, suddenly. I jumped unsteadily to my feet; I found my horse and rode away. I left Drieka Breytenbach where I had found her, under the thorn-tree by the roadside, with her hot whisperings still ringing in my ears, and before I reached home the moon had set behind the Dwarsberge.

Well, there is not much left for me to tell you. In the days that followed, Drieka Breytenbach was always in my thoughts. Her long, loose hair and her red lips and her feet that had been in the roadside sand with mine. But if she really was the ghost that I had at first taken her to be, I could not have been more afraid of her.

And it seemed singular that, while it had been my words, spoken in the moonlight, that helped to bring Drieka and me closer together, it was Drieka's hot breath, whispering wild words in my ear, that sent me so suddenly from her side.

Once or twice I even felt sorry for having left in that fashion.

And later on when I heard that Drieka Breytenbach had gone back to Schweizer-Reneke, and that her husband had been shot dead with his own Mauser by one of the farm kaffirs, I was not surprised. In fact, I had expected it.

Only it did not seem right, somehow, that Drieka should have got a kaffir to do the thing that I had refused to do.

Mampoer

THE berries of the kareeboom (Oom Schalk Lourens said, nodding his head in the direction of the tall tree whose shadows were creeping towards the edge of the stoep) may not make the best kind of mampoer that there is. What I mean is that karee brandy is not as potent as the brandy you distil from moepels or maroelas. Even peach brandy, they say, can make you forget the rust in the corn quicker than the mampoer you make from karee-berries.

But karee mampoer is white and soft to look at, and the smoke that comes from it when you pull the cork out of the bottle is pale and rises up in slow curves. And in time of drought, when you have been standing at the borehole all day, pumping water for the cattle, so that by the evening water has got a bitter taste for you, then it is very soothing to sit on the front stoep, like now, and to get somebody to pull the cork out of a bottle of this kind of mampoer. Your hands will be sore and stiff from the pump-handle, so that if you try and pull it out yourself the cork will seem as deep down in the bottle as the water is in the borehole.

Many years ago, when I was a young man, and I sat here, on the front stoep, and I saw that white smoke floating away slowly and gracefully from the mouth of the bottle, and with a far-off fragrance, I used to think that the smoke looked like a young girl walking veiled under the stars. And now that I have grown old, and I look at that white smoke, I imagine that it is a young girl walking under the stars, and still veiled. I have never found out who she is.

Hans Kriel and I were in the same party that had gone from this section of the Groot Marico to Zeerust for the Nagmaal. And it was a few evenings after our arrival, when we were on a visit to Kris Wilman's house on the outskirts of the town, that I learnt something of the first half of Hans Kriel's love story – that half at which I laughed. The knowledge of the second half came a little later, and I didn't laugh then.

We were sitting on Krisjan Wilman's stoep and looking out in the direction of Sephton's Nek. In the setting sun the koppies were red on one side; on the other side their shadows were lengthening rapidly over the vlakte. Krisjan Wilman had already poured out the mampoer, and the glasses were going round.

"That big shadow there is rushing through the thorn-trees just like a black elephant," Adriaan Bekker said. "In a few minutes' time it will be at Groot Marico station."

"The shorter the days are, the longer the shadows get," Frikkie Marais said. "I learnt that at school. There are also lucky and unlucky shadows."

"You are talking about ghosts, now, and not shadows," Adriaan Bekker interrupted him, learnedly. "Ghosts are all the same length, I think, more or less."

"No, it is the ghost stories that are all the same length," Krisjan Wilman said. "The kind you tell."

It was good mampoer, made from karee-berries that were plucked when they were still green and full of thick sap, just before they had begun to whiten, and we said things that contained much wisdom.

"It was like the shadow of a flower on her left cheek," I heard Hans Kriel say, and immediately I sat up to listen, for I could guess of what it was that he was talking.

"Is it on the lower part of her cheek?" I asked. "Two small purple marks?"

Because in that case I would know for sure that he was talking about the new waitress in the Zeerust café. I had seen her only once, through the plate-glass window, and because I had liked her looks I had gone up to the counter and asked her for a roll of Boer tobacco, which she said they did not stock. When she said they didn't stock koedoe biltong, either, I had felt too embarrassed to ask for anything else. Only afterwards I remembered that I could have gone in and sat down and ordered a cup of coffee and some harde beskuit. But it was too late then. By that time I felt that she could see that I came from this part of the Marico, even though I was wearing my hat well back on my head.

"Did you – did you speak to her?" I asked Hans Kriel after a while.

"Yes," he said, "I went in and asked her for a roll of Boer tobacco. But she said they didn't sell tobacco by the roll, or koedoe biltong, either. She said this last with a sort of a sneer. I thought it was funny, seeing that I hadn't asked her for koedoe biltong. So I sat down in front of a little table and ordered some harde beskuit and a cup of coffee. She brought me a number of little dry, flat cakes with letters on them that I couldn't read very well. Her name is Marie Rossouw."

"You must have said quite a lot to her to have found out her name," I said, with something in my voice that must have made Hans Kriel suspicious.

"How do you know who I am talking about?" he demanded suddenly.

"Oh, never mind," I answered. "Let us ask Krisjan Wilman to refill our glasses."

I winked at the others and we all laughed, because by that time Hans Kriel was sitting half-sideways on the riempies bench, with his shoulders drawn up very high and his whole body seeming to be kept up by one elbow. It wasn't long after that he moved his elbow, so that we had to pick him up from the floor and carry him into the voorkamer, where we laid him in a corner on some leopard skins.

But before that he had spoken more about Marie Rossouw, the new waitress in the café. He said he had passed by and had seen her through the plate-glass window and there had been a vase of purple flowers on the counter, and he had noticed those two marks on her cheek, and those marks had looked very pretty to him, like two small shadows from those purple flowers.

"She is very beautiful," Hans Kriel said. "Her eyes have got deep things in them, like those dark pools behind Abjaterskop. And when she smiled at me once – by mistake, I think – I felt as though my heart was rushing over the vlaktes like that shadow we saw in the sunset."

"You must be careful of those dark pools behind Abjaterskop," I warned him. "We know those pools have got witches in them."

I felt it was a pity that we had to carry him inside, shortly afterwards. For the mampoer had begun to make Hans Kriel talk rather well.

As it happened, Hans Kriel was not the only one, that night, who encountered difficulties with the riempies bench. Several more of us were carried inside. And when I look back on that Nagmaal my most vivid memories are not of what the predikant said at the church service, or of Krisjan Wilman's mampoer, even, but of how very round the black spots were on the pale yellow of the leopard skin. They were so round that every time I looked at them they were turning.

In the morning Krisjan Wilman's wife woke us up and brought us coffee. Hans Kriel and I sat up side by side on the leopard skins, and in between drinking his coffee Hans Kriel said strange things. He was still talking about Marie Rossouw.

"Just after dark I got up from the front stoep and went to see her in the café," Hans Kriel said.

"You may have got up from the front stoep," I answered, "but you never got up from these leopard skins. Not from the moment we carried you here. That's the truth."

"I went to the café," Hans Kriel said, ignoring my interruption, "and it was very dark. She was there alone. I wanted to find out how she got those marks on her cheek. I think she is very pretty even without them. But with those marks Marie Rossouw is the most wild and beautiful thing in the whole world."

"I suppose her cheek got cut there when she was a child," I suggested. "Perhaps when a bottle of her father's mampoer exploded."

"No," Hans Kriel replied, very earnestly. "No. It was something else. I asked her where the marks came from. I asked her there, in the café, where we were alone together, and it suddenly seemed as though the whole place was washed with moonlight, and there was no counter between us any more, and there was a strange laughter in her eyes when she brought her face very close to mine. And she said, 'I know you won't believe me. But that is where the devil kissed me. Satan kissed me there when we were behind Abjaterskop. Shall I show you?'

"That was what she said to me," Hans Kriel continued, "and I knew, then, that she was a witch. And that it was a very sinful thing to be in love with a witch. And so I caught her up in my arms, and I whispered, trembling all the time, 'Show me,' and our heads rose up very tall through the shadows. And everything moved very fast, faster than the shadows move from Abjaterskop in the setting of the sun. And I knew that we were behind Abjaterskop, and that her eyes were indeed the dark pools there, with the tall reeds growing on the edges. And then I saw Satan come in between us. And he had hooves and a forked tail. And there were flames coming out of him. And he stooped down and kissed Marie Rossouw, on her cheek, where those marks were. And she laughed. And her eyes danced with merriment. And I found that it was all the time I who was kissing her. Now, what do you make of this, Schalk?"

I said, of course, that it was the mampoer. And that I knew, now, why I had been sleeping in such discomfort. It wasn't because the spots on the leopard skin were turning like round wheels; but because I had Satan sleeping next to me all night. And I said that this discovery wasn't new, either. I had always suspected something like that about him.

But I got an idea. And while the others were at breakfast I went out, on the pretext that I had to go and help Manie Burgers with his oxen at the church square outspan. But, instead, I went into the café, and because I knew her name was Marie Rossouw, when the waitress came for my order I could ask her whether she was related to the Rossouws of Rysmierbult, and I could tell her that I was distantly related to that family, also. In the daylight there was about that café none of the queerness that Hans Kriel had spoken about. It was all very ordinary. Even those purple flowers were still on the counter. They looked slightly faded.

And then, suddenly, while we were talking, I asked her the thing that I was burning to know.

"That mark on your cheek, juffrou," I said, "will you tell me where you got it from?"

Marie Rossouw brought her face very close to mine, and her eyes were like dark pools with dancing lights in them.

"I know you won't believe me," she said, "but that is where Satan kissed me. When we were at the back of Abjaterskop together. Shall I show you?"

It was broad daylight. The morning lay yellow on the world and the sun shone in brightly through the plate-glass window, and there were quite a number of people in the street. And yet as I walked out of the café quickly, and along the pavement, I was shivering.

With one thing and another, I did not come across Hans Kriel again until three or four days later, when the Nagmaal was over and we were trekking to the other side of the Dwarsberge once more.

We spoke of a number of things, and then, trying to make my voice sound natural, I made mention of Marie Rossouw.

"That was a queer sort of dream you had," I said.

"Yes," he answered, "it was queer."

"And did you find out," I asked, again trying to sound casual, "about those marks on her cheek?"

"Yes," Hans Kriel answered, "I asked Marie and she told me. She said that when she was a child a bottle of mampoer burst in the voorkamer. Her cheek got cut by a splinter of glass. She is an unusual kind of girl, Marie Rossouw."

"Yes," I agreed, moving away. "Oh, yes."

But I also thought that there are things about mampoer that you can't understand very easily.

The Widow

THERE had been no rain in the Potchefstroom District for many months, and so the ground was very hard that morning, and the picks and shovels of the kaffirs rang on the gravel, by the side of the mud hut that had been used as a courthouse.

I was a boy then. It was at the time when the Transvaal was divided into four separate republics, and Potchefstroom, which was a small village, was the capital of the southern republic.

For several days there had been much activity in the courthouse. From distant parts the farmers had come to attend the trial of Tjaart van Rensburg. Only a few could get inside the court. The rest watched at the door, crowding forward eagerly after each witness had stepped down from the stand; those inside told them what evidence had been given.

Naturally there was much excitement over these court proceedings, and in Potchefstroom people talked of little else but the Transvaal's first murder trial.

The whole thing started when Andries Theron was found beside the borehole on his farm. He had been pumping water for his cattle. One Rossouw, a neighbour of Andries Theron's, passing by in his ox-wagon, saw a man lying next to the pump-handle.

Thus it was that Francina Theron saw her husband arrive home in a stranger's ox-wagon, with a piece of bucksail pulled over his body, and a Martini bullet in his heart. The landdrost's men came from Potchefstroom and proceeded to investigate the murder, spending much of their time, as landdrosts' men always do, in trying to frighten the wrong people into confessing.

But afterwards they got their information.

They say there was a large crowd at the funeral of Andries Theron, which took place at the foot of a koppie on the far end of his farm. They came, the women in black clothes and the men in their Sunday hats; and in that sad procession that wound slowly over the veld, following the wagon with the coffin on it, there were also two landdrost's men.

Among the mourners was the dead man's cousin, Tjaart van Rensburg. The minister did not take long over the funeral service. He

115

said a few simple words about the tragic way in which Andries Theron had died, adding that no man knew when his hour was come. He then spoke a brief message of comfort to the widow, Francina, and offered up a prayer for the dead man's soul.

The last notes of the Boer hymn had died on the veld, and the crowd had already begun to move away from the graveside, when one of the landdrost's men put his hand on Tjaart van Rensburg's shoulder. With an officer of the law on each side of him, the fetters on his wrists, Tjaart van Rensburg led the procession down the stony road.

The prisoner had turned very pale. But they all noticed that his head was erect and his step firm, when he walked to the bluegum trees on the other side of the hill, where the Government Cape-cart waited.

A month later the trial commenced in Potchefstroom.

Andries Theron's widow, Francina, was a slenderly-built woman, still in her early twenties. She had been very pretty at one time, with light-hearted ways and a merry laugh. But the shock of her husband's death had changed her in an hour. She did not weep when Rossouw, who had a good heart but blunt ways, informed her that he had found her husband lying dead on the veld.

"I was lucky," Rossouw said, "to have found him before the vultures did."

"Where is he?" Francina asked.

"On my wagon," Rossouw answered, "under the first bucksail you come to. Next to the sacks of potatoes."

In some respects Rossouw did not have what you would call a real delicacy of feeling. But he possessed a sombre thing of the veld, which told him that he must not follow Francina to the wagon, because it was right that, at her first meeting with her dead husband, a wife should be alone.

Francina was at the wagon a long time.

When she came back she was sadly changed. The colour had left her cheeks and her lips. Her mouth sagged at the corners. But in her tear-less eyes there was a lost and hopeless look, a dreadful desolation that frightened Rossouw when he saw it, so that he made no effort to comfort her.

It was the same with the women who came to console Francina. If a woman wanted to take Francina in her arms, so that she could weep on her bosom, there was that look in her eyes that spoke of a sorrow that must be for always.

You can't do much, if all you have to offer a widow is human sympathy, and she looks back at you with wide eyes that seem to want nothing more from this world or the world to come. You get uneasy, then, and feel that you have no right to trespass on this sort of sorrow.

That was what happened to the women who knew Francina. They were kind to her in little ways. When the time for the murder trial came, and it seemed likely that Francina would be called as a witness, a woman accompanied her to Potchefstroom and stayed with her there. But even to this woman, in her grief, Francina remained a stranger.

In fact, this woman always said, afterwards, that during all the time she was with her, Francina spoke to her only once; and that was when they were at the Mooi River, which flows through Potchefstroom, and Francina said how pretty the yellow flowers grew on the banks of the river.

So the trial began. Every morning, at nine o'clock, Tjaart van Rensburg was led from the gaol to the courthouse with the mud walls. There were always many people standing around to see him pass. I saw him quite often. The impression I get, when I look back to that time, is that Tjaart van Rensburg was a broad-shouldered man of about thirty, taller than the guards who escorted him, and rather good-looking.

I remember the way he walked, with his head up, and his hat on a slant, and his wrists close together in front of him. On each side of him was a burgher with a bandolier and a rifle.

The landdrost looked important, as a landdrost should look at his first murder trial. The jurymen also looked very dignified. But the most pompous of all was Rossouw. Over and over again, to anyone who would listen, he told the story of how he discovered the body before the vultures did. He told everybody just what evidence he was going to give, and what theories he was going to put forward as to how the murder was committed.

He even brought his ox-wagon along to the courthouse and drew it up on the sidewalk, so that the landdrost and the jurymen had difficulty in getting in at the door. He said he was willing to demonstrate to the court just at what pace he drove the body from the borehole to Andries Theron's house.

Afterwards, Rossouw was the most disappointed man I ever saw. For he was only kept in the witness-box for about five minutes, and they wouldn't listen to any of his theories.

On the other hand, a kaffir, who saw Tjaart van Rensburg arguing with the deceased in front of the borehole, gave evidence for over three hours. And another kaffir, who heard a shot and thought he saw Tjaart van Rensburg running down the road with a gun, was in the witness-box for the best part of a day.

"What do you think of this for a piece of nonsense?" Rossouw asked of a group standing about the courthouse. "I am a white man. I have borne arms for the Transvaal in three kaffir wars. And I am only in the witness-box for five minutes, when they tell me to step down and move my ox-wagon away from the door. And yet a raw kaffir, who can't even sign his name, but has got to put a cross at the foot of the things he has said – this raw kaffir is allowed to stand there wasting the time of the court for ten hours on end.

"What's more," Rossouw went on, "Tjaart van Rensburg's lawyer never once cross-questioned me or called me a liar. Whereas he spent half a day in calling that kaffir names. Doesn't that lawyer think that my evidence is of any value to the court?"

Rossouw said a lot more things like that. Some of the burghers laughed at his remarks, but others took him seriously, and agreed with him, and said it was a shame that such things should be allowed, and that it all proved that the president did not have the interests of the nation at heart.

You can see, from this, that it must have been a difficult task to govern the Transvaal in those days.

The case lasted almost a week, what with all the witnesses, and the long speeches made by the prosecution and the defence. Also, the land-drost said a great many learned things about the Roman-Dutch law. During all this time Francina sat in court with that same unearthly look in her eyes. They say that she never once wept. Even when the doctor, a Hollander, explained how he cut open Andries Theron's body, and found that the bullet had gone through his heart, the expression on Francina's face did not change.

People who knew her grew anxious about her state. They said it was impossible for her to continue in this way, with that stony grief inside her. They said that if she did not break down and weep she could not go on living much longer.

Anyway, Francina was not called as a witness. Perhaps they felt that there was nothing of importance that she could say.

So the days passed.

And Rossouw was still complaining about the unfair way he had been treated in the witness-box, when Tjaart van Rensburg, his hat tilted over the eye and his wrists close together in front of him, strode into the courthouse for the last time.

The landdrost looked less important on that morning. And the jurymen did not seem very happy. But they were not the kind of men to shirk a duty they had sworn to carry out.

Tjaart van Rensburg was asked if he had anything to say before sentence was passed on him.

"Yes, I am guilty," he answered. "I shot Andries Theron."

His voice was steady, and as he spoke he twirled the brim of his hat slowly round and round between his fingers.

And that was how it came about that, early one winter's morning, a number of kaffirs were swinging their picks into the hard gravel, digging a hole by the side of the courthouse.

A small group had gathered at the graveside. Some were kneeling in prayer. Among the spectators was Francina Theron, looking very frail and slender in her widow's weeds. When the grave was deep enough a roughly-constructed coffin was lifted out of a cart that bore, painted on its side, the arms of the republic.

The grave was filled in. The newly-made mound of gravel and red earth was patted smooth with the shovels.

Then, for the first time since her husband's death, Francina wept.

She flung herself at full-length on the mound, and trailed her fingers through the pebbles and fresh earth. And calling out tender and passionate endearments, Francina sobbed noisily on the grave of her lover.

Veld Maiden

KNOW what it is – Oom Schalk Lourens said – when you talk that way about the veld. I have known people who sit like you do and dream about the veld, and talk strange things, and start believing in what they call the soul of the veld, until in the end the veld means a different thing to them from what it does to me.

I only know that the veld can be used for growing mealies on, and it isn't very good for that, either. Also, it means very hard work for me, growing mealies. There is the ploughing, for instance. I used to get aches in my back and shoulders from sitting on a stone all day long on the edge of the lands, watching the kaffirs and the oxen and the plough going up and down, making furrows. Hans Coetzee, who was a Boer War prisoner at St. Helena, told me how he got sick at sea from watching the ship going up and down, up and down, all the time.

And it's the same with ploughing. The only real cure for this ploughing sickness is to sit quietly on a riempies bench on the stoep, with one's legs raised slightly, drinking coffee until the ploughing season is over. Most of the farmers in the Marico Bushveld have adopted this remedy, as you have no doubt observed by this time.

But there the veld is. And it is not good to think too much about it. For then it can lead you in strange ways. And sometimes – sometimes when the veld has led you very far – there comes into your eyes a look that God did not put there.

It was in the early summer, shortly after the rains, that I first came across John de Swardt. He was sitting next to a tent that he had pitched behind the maroelas at the far end of my farm, where it adjoins Frans Welman's lands. He had been there several days and I had not known about it, because I sat much on my stoep then, on account of what I have already explained to you about the ploughing.

He was a young fellow with long black hair. When I got nearer I saw what he was doing. He had a piece of white bucksail on a stand in front of him and he painting my farm. He seemed to have picked out all the useless bits for his picture – a krantz and a few stones and some clumps of kakiebos.

"Young man," I said to him, after we had introduced ourselves, "when people in Johannesburg see that picture they will laugh and say that Schalk Lourens lives on a barren piece of rock, like a lizard does. Why don't you rather paint the fertile parts? Look at that vlei there, and the dam. And put in that new cattle-dip that I have just built up with reinforced concrete. Then, if Piet Grobler or General Kemp sees this picture, he will know at once that Schalk Lourens has been making improvements on the farm."

The young painter shook his head.

"No," he said, "I want to paint only the veld. I hate the idea of painting boreholes and cattle-dips and houses and concrete – especially concrete. I want only the veld. Its loneliness. Its mystery. When this picture is finished I'll be proud to put my name to it."

"Oh, well, that is different," I replied, "as long as you don't put my name to it. Better still," I said, "put Frans Welman's name to it. Write underneath that this is Frans Welman's farm."

I said that because I still remembered that Frans Welman had voted against me at the last election of the Drogekop School Committee.

John de Swardt then took me into his tent and showed me some other pictures he had painted at different places along the Dwarsberge. They were all the same sort of picture, barren and stony. I thought it would be a good idea if the Government put up a lot of pictures like that on the Kalahari border for the locusts to see. Because that would keep the locusts out of the Marico.

Then John de Swardt showed me another picture he had painted and when I saw that I got a different opinion about this thing that he said was Art. I looked from De Swardt to the picture and then back again to De Swardt.

"I'd never have thought it of you," I said, "and you look such a quiet sort, too."

"I call it the 'Veld Maiden'," John de Swardt said.

"If the predikant saw it he'd call it by other names," I replied. "But I am a broad-minded man. I have been once in the bar in Zeerust and twice in the bioscope when I should have been attending Nagmaal. So I don't hold it against a young man for having ideas like this. But you mustn't let anybody here see this Veld Maiden unless you paint a few more clothes on her."

"I couldn't," De Swardt answered, "that's just how I see her. That's just how I dream about her. For many years now she has come to me so in my dreams."

"With her arms stretched out like that?" I asked.

121

"Yes."

"And with – "

"Yes, yes, just like that," De Swardt said very quickly. Then he blushed and I could see how very young he was. It seemed a pity that a nice young fellow like that should be so mad.

"Anyway, if ever you want a painting job," I said when I left, "you can come and whitewash the back of my sheep-kraal."

I often say funny things like that to people.

I saw a good deal of John de Swardt after that, and I grew to like him. I was satisfied – in spite of his wasting his time in painting bare stones and weeds – that there was no real evil in him. I was sure that he only talked silly things about visions and the spirit of the veld because of what they had done to him at the school in Johannesburg where they taught him all that nonsense about art, and I felt sorry for him. Afterwards I wondered for a little while if I shouldn't rather have felt sorry for the art school. But when I had thought it all out carefully I knew that John de Swardt was only very young and innocent, and that what happened to him later on was the sort of thing that does happen to those who are simple of heart.

On several Sundays in succession I took De Swardt over the rant to the house of Frans Welman. I hadn't a very high regard for Frans's judgment since the time he voted for the wrong man at the School Committee. But I had no other neighbour within walking distance, and I had to go somewhere on a Sunday.

We talked of all sorts of things. Frans's wife Sannie was young and pretty, but very shy. She wasn't naturally like that. It was only that she was afraid to talk in case she said something of which her husband might disapprove. So most of the time Sannie sat silent in the corner, getting up now and again to make more coffee for us.

Frans Welman was in some respects what people might call a hard man. For instance, it was something of a mild scandal the way he treated his wife and the kaffirs on his farm. But then, on the other hand, he looked very well after his cattle and pigs. And I have always believed that this is more important in a farmer than that he should be kind to his wife and the kaffirs.

Well, we talked about the mealies and the drought of the year before last and the subsidies, and I could see that in a short while the conversation would come round to the Volksraad, and as I wasn't anxious to hear how Frans was going to vote at the General Election – believing that so irresponsible a person should not be allowed to vote at all – I quickly asked John de Swardt to tell us about his paintings.

Immediately he started off about his Veld Maiden.

"Not that one," I said, kicking his shin, "I meant your other paintings. The kind that frighten the locusts."

I felt that this Veld Maiden thing was not a fit subject to talk about, especially with a woman present. Moreover, it was Sunday.

Nevertheless, that kick came too late. De Swardt rubbed his shin a few times and started on his subject, and although Frans and I cleared our throats awkwardly at different parts, and Sannie looked on the floor with her pretty cheeks very red, the young painter explained everything about that picture and what it meant to him.

"It's a dream I have had for a long time, now," he said at the end, "and always she comes to me, and when I put out my arms to clasp her to me she vanishes, and I am left with only her memory in my heart. But when she comes the whole world is clothed in a terrible beauty."

"That's more than she is clothed in, anyway," Frans said, "judging from what you have told us about her."

"She's a spirit. She's the spirit of the veld," De Swardt murmured, "she whispers strange and enchanting things. Her coming is like the whisper of the wind. She's not of the earth at all."

"Oh, well," Frans said shortly, "you can keep these Uitlander ghost-women of yours. A Boer girl is good enough for ordinary fellows like me and Schalk Lourens."

So the days passed.

John de Swardt finished a few more bits of rock and drought-stricken kakiebos, and I had got so far as to persuade him to label the worst-looking one "Frans Welman's Farm."

Then one morning he came to me in great excitement.

"I saw her again, Oom Schalk," he said, "I saw her last night. In a surpassing loveliness. Just at midnight. She came softly across the veld towards my tent. The night was warm and lovely, and the stars were mad and singing. And there was low music where her white feet touched the grass. And sometimes her mouth seemed to be laughing, and sometimes it was sad. And her lips were very red, Oom Schalk. And when I reached out with my arms she went away. She disappeared in the maroelas, like the whispering of the wind. And there was a ringing in my ears. And in my heart there was a green fragrance, and I thought of the pale asphodel that grows in the fields of paradise."

"I don't know about paradise," I said, "but if a thing like that grew in my mealie-lands I would see to it at once that the kaffirs pulled it up. I don't like this spook nonsense."

I then gave him some good advice. I told him to beware of the moon, which was almost full at the time. Because the moon can do strange things to you in the Bushveld, especially if you live in a tent and the full moon is overhead and there are weird shadows amongst the maroelas.

But I knew he wouldn't take any notice of what I told him.

Several times after that he came with the same story about the Veld Maiden. I started getting tired of it.

Then, one morning when he came again, I knew everything by the look he had in his eyes. I have already told you about that look.

"Oom Schalk," he began.

"John de Swardt," I said to him, "don't tell me anything. All I ask of you is to pack up your things and leave my farm at once."

"I'll leave tonight," he said. "I promise you that by tomorrow morning I will be gone. Only let me stay here one more day and night."

His voice trembled when he spoke, and his knees were very unsteady. But it was not for these reasons or for his sake that I relented. I spoke to him civilly for the sake of the look he had in his eyes.

"Very well, then," I said, "but you must go straight back to Johannesburg. If you walk down the road you will be able to catch the Government lorry to Zeerust."

He thanked me and left. I never saw him again.

Next day his tent was still there behind the maroelas, but John de Swardt was gone, and he had taken with him all his pictures. All, that is, except the Veld Maiden one. I suppose he had no more need for it.

And, in any case, the white ants had already started on it. So that's why I can hang the remains of it openly on the wall in my voorhuis, and the predikant does not raise any objection to it. For the white ants have eaten away practically all of it except the face.

As for Frans Welman, it was quite a long time before he gave up searching the Marico for his young wife, Sannie.

The Rooinek

ROOINEKS, said Oom Schalk Lourens, are queer. For instance, there was that day when my nephew Hannes and I had dealings with a couple of Englishmen near Dewetsdorp. It was shortly after Sanna's Post, and Hannes and I were lying behind a rock watching the road. Hannes spent odd moments like that in what he called a useful way. He would file the points of his Mauser cartridges on a piece of flat stone until the lead showed through the steel, in that way making them into dum-dum bullets.

I often spoke to my nephew Hannes about that.

"Hannes," I used to say. "That is a sin. The Lord is looking at you."

"That's all right," Hannes replied. "The Lord knows that this is the Boer War, and in war-time he will always forgive a little foolishness like this, especially as the English are so many."

Anyway, as we lay behind that rock we saw, far down the road, two horsemen come galloping up. We remained perfectly still and let them approach to within four hundred paces. They were English officers. They were mounted on first-rate horses and their uniforms looked very fine and smart. They were the most stylish-looking men I had seen for some time, and I felt quite ashamed of my own ragged trousers and veldskoens. I was glad that I was behind a rock and they couldn't see me. Especially as my jacket was also torn all the way down the back, as a result of my having had, three days before, to get through a barbed-wire fence rather quickly. I just got through in time, too. The veldkornet, who was a fat man and couldn't run so fast, was about twenty yards behind me. And he remained on the wire with a bullet through him. All through the Boer War I was pleased that I was thin and never troubled with corns.

Hannes and I fired just about the same time. One of the officers fell off his horse. He struck the road with his shoulders and rolled over twice, kicking up the red dust as he turned. Then the other soldier did a queer thing. He drew up his horse and got off. He gave just one look in our direction. Then he led his horse up to where the other man was twisting and struggling on the ground. It took him a little while to lift him on to his horse, for it is no easy matter to pick up a man like that when he is helpless. And he did all this slowly and calmly, as though he was not concerned about the fact that the men who had shot his friend were lying only a few hundred yards away. He managed in some way to support the wounded man across the saddle, and walked on beside the horse. After going a few yards he stopped and seemed to remember something. He turned round and waved at the spot where he imagined we were hiding, as though inviting us to shoot. During all that time I had simply lain watching him, astonished at his coolness.

But when he waved his hand I thrust another cartridge into the breach of my Martini and aimed. At that distance I couldn't miss. I aimed very carefully and was just on the point of pulling the trigger when Hannes put his hand on the barrel and pushed up my rifle.

"Don't shoot, Oom Schalk," he said. "That's a brave man."

I looked at Hannes in surprise. His face was very white. I said nothing, and allowed my rifle to sink down on to the grass, but I couldn't understand what had come over my nephew. It seemed that not only was that Englishman queer, but that Hannes was also queer. That's all nonsense not killing a man just because he's brave. If he's a brave man and he's fighting on the wrong side, that's all the more reason to shoot him.

I was with my nephew Hannes for another few months after that. Then one day, in a skirmish near the Vaal River, Hannes with a few dozen other burghers was cut off from the commando and had to surrender. That was the last I ever saw of him. I heard later on that, after taking him prisoner, the English searched Hannes and found dum-dum bullets in his possession. They shot him for that. I was very much grieved when I heard of Hannes's death. He had always been full of life and high spirits. Perhaps Hannes was right in saying that the Lord didn't mind about a little foolishness like dum-dum bullets. But the mistake he made was in forgetting that the English did mind.

I was in the veld until they made peace. Then we laid down our rifles and went home. What I knew my farm by was the hole under the koppie where I quarried slate-stones for the threshing-floor. That was about all that remained as I left it. Everything else was gone. My home was burnt down. My lands were laid waste. My cattle and sheep were slaughtered. Even the stones I had piled for the kraals were pulled down. My wife came out of the concentration camp, and we went together to look at our old farm. My wife had gone into the concentration camp with our two children, but she came out alone. And when I saw her again and noticed the way she had changed, I knew that I, who had been through all the fighting, had not seen the Boer War.

Neither Sannie nor I had the heart to go on farming again on that same place. It would be different without the children playing about the house and getting into mischief. We got paid out some money by the new Government for part of our losses. So I bought a wagon and oxen and left the Free State, which was not even the Free State any longer. It was now called the Orange River Colony.

We trekked right through the Transvaal into the northern part of the Marico Bushveld. Years ago, as a boy, I had trekked through that same country with my parents. Now that I went there again I felt that it was still a good country. It was on the far side of the Dwarsberge, near Derdepoort, that we got a Government farm. Afterwards other farmers trekked in there as well. One or two of them had also come from the Free State, and I knew them. There were also a few Cape rebels whom I had seen on commando. All of us had lost relatives in the war. Some had died in the concentration camps or on the battlefield. Others had been shot for going into rebellion. So, taken all in all, we who had trekked into that part of the Marico that lay nearest the Bechuanaland border were very bitter against the English.

Then it was that the rooinek came.

It was in the first year of our having settled around Derdepoort. We heard that an Englishman had bought a farm next to Gerhardus Grobbelaar. This was when we were sitting in the voorkamer of Willem Odendaal's house, which was used as a post office. Once a week the post-cart came up with letters from Zeerust, and we came together at Willem Odendaal's house and talked and smoked and drank coffee. Very few of us ever got letters, and then it was mostly demands to pay for the boreholes that had been drilled on our farms or for cement and fencing materials. But every week regularly we went for the post. Sometimes the post-cart didn't come, because the Groen River was in flood, and we would most of us have gone home without noticing it, if somebody didn't speak about it.

When Koos Steyn heard that an Englishman was coming to live amongst us he got up from the riempies-bank.

"No, kêrels," he said. "Always when the Englishman comes, it means that a little later the Boer has got to shift. I'll pack up my wagon and make coffee, and just trek first thing tomorrow morning."

Most of us laughed then. Koos Steyn often said funny things like that. But some didn't laugh. Somehow, there seemed to be too much truth in Koos Steyn's words.

We discussed the matter and decided that if we Boers in the Marico could help it the rooinek would not stay amongst us too long. About half an hour later one of Willem Odendaal's children came in and said that there was a strange wagon coming along the big road. We went to the door and looked out. As the wagon came nearer we saw that it was piled up with all kinds of furniture and also sheets of iron and farming implements. There was so much stuff on the wagon that the tent had to be taken off to get everything on.

The wagon rolled along and came to a stop in front of the house. With the wagon there were one white man and two kaffirs. The white man shouted something to the kaffirs and threw down the whip. Then he walked up to where we were standing. He was dressed just as we were, in shirt and trousers and veldskoens, and he had dust all over him. But when he stepped over a thorn-bush we saw that he had got socks on. Therefore we knew that he was an Englishman.

Koos Steyn was standing in front of the door.

The Englishman went up to him and held out his hand.

"Good afternoon," he said in Afrikaans. "My name is Webber."

Koos shook hands with him.

"My name is Prince Lord Alfred Milner," Koos Steyn said.

That was when Lord Milner was Governor of the Transvaal, and we all laughed. The rooinek also laughed.

"Well, Lord Prince," he said, "I can speak your language a little, and I hope that later on I'll be able to speak it better. I'm coming to live here, and I hope that we'll all be friends."

He then came round to all of us, but the others turned away and refused to shake hands with him. He came up to me last of all; I felt sorry for him, and although his nation had dealt unjustly with my nation, and I had lost both my children in the concentration camp, still it was not so much the fault of this Englishman. It was the fault of the English Government, who wanted our gold mines. And it was also the fault of Queen Victoria, who didn't like Oom Paul Kruger, because they say that when he went over to London Oom Paul spoke to her only once for a few minutes. Oom Paul Kruger said that he was a married man and he was afraid of widows.

When the Englishman Webber went back to his wagon Koos Steyn and I walked with him. He told us that he had bought the farm next to Gerhardus Grobbelaar and that he didn't know much about sheep and cattle and mealies, but he had bought a few books on farming, and he was going to learn all he could out of them. When he said that I looked away towards the poort. I didn't want him to see that I was laughing. But with Koos Steyn it was otherwise.

"Man," he said, "let me see those books."

Webber opened the box at the bottom of the wagon and took out about six big books with green covers.

"These are very good books," Koos Steyn said. "Yes, they are very good for the white ants. The white ants will eat them all in two nights."

As I have told you, Koos Steyn was a funny fellow, and no man could help laughing at the things he said.

Those were bad times. There was drought, and we could not sow mealies. The dams dried up, and there was only last year's grass on the veld. We had to pump water out of the borehole for weeks at a time. Then the rains came and for a while things were better.

Now and again I saw Webber. From what I heard about him it seemed that he was working hard. But of course no rooinek can make a living out of farming, unless they send him money every month from England. And we found out that almost all the money Webber had was what he had paid on the farm. He was always reading in those green books what he had to do. It's lucky that those books are written in English, and that the Boers can't read them. Otherwise many more farmers would be ruined every year. When his cattle had the heart-water, or his sheep had the blue-tongue, or there were cut-worms or stalk-borers in his mealies, Webber would look it all up in his books. I suppose that when the kaffirs stole his sheep he would look that up too.

Still, Koos Steyn helped Webber quite a lot and taught him a number of things, so that matters did not go as badly with him as they would have if he had only acted according to the lies that were printed in those green books. Webber and Koos Steyn became very friendly. Koos Steyn's wife had had a baby just a few weeks before Webber came. It was the first child they had after being married seven years, and they were very proud of it. It was a girl. Koos Steyn said that he would sooner it had been a boy; but that, even so, it was better than nothing. Right from the first Webber had taken a liking to that child, who was christened Jemima after her mother. Often when I passed Koos Steyn's house I saw the Englishman sitting on the front stoep with the child on his knees.

In the meantime the other farmers around there became annoyed on account of Koos Steyn's friendship with the rooinek. They said that Koos was a hendsopper and a traitor to his country. He was intimate with a man who had helped to bring about the downfall of the Afrikaner nation. Yet it was not fair to call Koos a hendsopper. Koos had lived in the Graaff-Reinet District when the war broke out, so that he was a Cape Boer and need not have fought. Nevertheless, he joined up with a Free State commando and remained until peace was made, and if at any time the English had caught him they would have shot him as a rebel, in the same way that they shot Scheepers and many others.

Gerhardus Grobbelaar spoke about this once when we were in Willem Odendaal's post office.

"You are not doing right," Gerhardus said; "Boer and Englishman have been enemies since before Slagtersnek. We've lost this war, but some day we'll win. It's the duty we owe to our children's children to stand against the rooineks. Remember the concentration camps."

There seemed to me to be truth in what Gerhardus said.

"But the English are here now, and we've got to live with them," Koos answered. "When we get to understand one another perhaps we won't need to fight any more. This Englishman Webber is learning Afrikaans very well, and some day he might almost be one of us. The only thing I can't understand about him is that he has a bath every morning. But if he stops that and if he doesn't brush his teeth any more you will hardly be able to tell him from a Boer."

Although he made a joke about it, I felt that in what Koos Steyn said there was also truth.

Then, the year after the drought, the miltsiek broke out. The miltsiek seemed to be in the grass of the veld, and in the water of the dams, and even in the air the cattle breathed. All over the place I would find cows and oxen lying dead. We all became very discouraged. Nearly all of us in that part of the Marico had started farming again on what the Government had given us. Now that the stock died we had nothing. First the drought had put us back to where we were when we started. Now with the miltsiek we couldn't hope to do anything. We couldn't even sow mealies, because, at the rate at which the cattle were dying, in a short while we would have no oxen left to pull the plough. People talked of selling what they had and going to look for work on the gold mines. We sent a petition to the Government, but that did no good.

It was then that somebody got hold of the idea of trekking. In a few days we were talking of nothing else. But the question was where we could trek to. They would not allow us into Rhodesia for fear we might spread the miltsiek there as well. And it was useless going to any other part of the Transvaal. Somebody mentioned German West Africa. We had none of us been there before, and I suppose that really was the reason why, in the end, we decided to go there.

"The blight of the English is over South Africa," Gerhardus Grobbelaar said. "We'll remain here only to die. We must go away somewhere where there is not the Englishman's flag."

In a few weeks' time we arranged everything. We were going to trek across the Kalahari into German territory. Everything we had we loaded up. We drove the cattle ahead and followed behind on our wagons. There were five families: the Steyns, the Grobbelaars, the Odendaals, the Ferreiras and Sannie and I. Webber also came with us. I think it was not so much that he was anxious to leave as that he and Koos Steyn had become very much attached to one another, and the Englishman did not wish to remain alone behind.

The youngest person in our trek was Koos Steyn's daughter Jemima, who was then about eighteen months old. Being the baby, she was a favourite with all of us.

Webber sold his wagon and went with Koos Steyn's trek.

When at the end of the first day we outspanned several miles inside the Bechuanaland Protectorate, we were very pleased that we were done with the Transvaal, where we had had so much misfortune. Of course, the Protectorate was also British territory, but all the same we felt happier there than we had done in our country. We saw Webber every day now, and although he was a foreigner with strange ways, and would remain an Uitlander until he died, yet we disliked him less than before for being a rooinek.

It was on the first Sunday that we reached Malopolole. For the first part of our way the country remained Bushveld. There were the same kind of thorn-trees that grew in the Marico, except that they became fewer the deeper into the Kalahari that we went. Also, the ground became more and more sandy, until even before we came to Malopolole it was all desert. But scattered thorn-bushes remained all the way. That Sunday we held a religious service. Gerhardus Grobbelaar read a chapter out of the Bible and offered up a prayer. We sang a number of psalms, after which Gerhardus prayed again. I shall always remember that Sunday and the way we sat on the ground beside one of the wagons, listening to Gerhardus. That was the last Sunday that we were all together.

The Englishman sat next to Koos Steyn and the baby Jemima lay down in front of him. She played with Webber's fingers and tried to bite them. It was funny to watch her. Several times Webber looked down at her and smiled. I thought then that although Webber was not one of us, yet Jemima certainly did not know it. Maybe in a thing like that the child was wiser than we were. To her it made no difference that the man whose fingers she bit was born in another country and did not speak the same language that she did.

There are many things that I remember about that trek into the Kalahari. But one thing that now seems strange to me is the way in which, right from the first day, we took Gerhardus Grobbelaar for our leader. Whatever he said we just seemed to do without talking very much about it. We all felt that it was right simply because Gerhardus wished it. That was a strange thing about our trek. It was not simply that we knew Gerhardus had got the Lord with him – for we did know that – but it was rather that we believed in Gerhardus as well as in the Lord. I think that even if Gerhardus Grobbelaar had been an ungodly man we would still have followed him in exactly the same way. For when you are in the desert and there is no water and the way back is long, then you feel that it is better to have with you a strong man who does not read the Book very much, than a man who is good and religious, and yet does not seem sure how far to trek each day and where to outspan.

But Gerhardus Grobbelaar was a man of God. At the same time there was something about him that made you feel that it was only by acting as he advised that you could succeed. There was only one other man I have ever known who found it so easy to get people to do as he wanted. And that was Paul Kruger. He was very much like Gerhardus Grobbelaar, except that Gerhardus was less quarrelsome. But of the two Paul Kruger was the bigger man.

Only once do I remember Gerhardus losing his temper. And that was with the Nagmaal at Elandsberg. It was on a Sunday, and we were camped out beside the Crocodile River. Gerhardus went round early in the morning from wagon to wagon and told us that he wanted everybody to come over to where his wagon stood. The Lord had been good to us at that time, so that we had had much rain and our cattle were fat. Gerhardus explained that he wanted to hold a service, to thank the Lord for all His good works, but more especially for what He had done for the farmers of the northern part of the Groot Marico District. This was a good plan, and we all came together with our Bibles and hymnbooks. But one man, Karel Pieterse, remained behind at his wagon. Twice Gerhardus went to call him, but Karel Pieterse lay down on the grass and would not get up to come to the service. He said it was all right thanking the Lord now that there had been rains, but what about all those seasons when there had been drought and the cattle had died of thirst. Gerhardus Grobbelaar shook his head sadly, and said there was nothing he could do then, as it was Sunday. But he prayed that the Lord would soften Brother Pieterse's heart, and he finished off his prayer by saying that in any case, in the morning, he would help to soften the brother's heart himself.

The following morning Gerhardus walked over with a sjambok and an ox-riem to where Karel Pieterse sat before his fire, watching the kaffir making coffee. They were both of them men who were big in the body. But Gerhardus got the better of the struggle. In the end he won. He fastened Karel to the wheel of his own wagon with the ox-riem. Then he thrashed him with the sjambok while Karel's wife and children were looking on.

That had happened years before. But nobody had forgotten. And now, in the Kalahari, when Gerhardus summoned us to a service, it was noticed that no man stayed away.

Just outside Malopolole is a muddy stream that is dry part of the year and part of the year has a foot or so of brackish water. We were lucky in being there just at the time when it had water. Early the following morning we filled up the water-barrels that we had put on our wagons before leaving the Marico. We were going right into the desert, and we did not know where we would get water again. Even the Bakwena kaffirs could not tell us for sure.

"The Great Dorstland Trek," Koos Steyn shouted as we got ready to move off. "Anyway, we won't fare as badly as the Dorstland Trekkers.

We'll lose less cattle than they did because we've got less to lose. And seeing that we are only five families, not more than about a dozen of us will die of thirst."

I thought it was bad luck for Koos Steyn to make jokes like that about the Dorstland Trek, and I think that others felt the same way about it. We trekked right through that day, and it was all desert. By sunset we had not come across a sign of water anywhere. Abraham Ferreira said towards evening that perhaps it would be better if we went back to Malopolole and tried to find out for sure which was the best way of getting through the Kalahari. But the rest said that there was no need to do that, since we would be sure to come across water the next day. And, anyway, we were Doppers and, having once set out, we were not going to turn back. But after we had given the cattle water our barrels did not have too much left in them.

By the middle of the following day all our water had given out except a little that we kept for the children. But still we pushed on. Now that we had gone so far we were afraid to go back because of the long way that we would have to go without water to get back to Malopolole. In the evening we were very anxious. We all knelt down in the sand and prayed. Gerhardus Grobbelaar's voice sounded very deep and earnest when he besought God to have mercy on us, especially for the sakes of the little ones. He mentioned the baby Jemima by name. The Englishman knelt down beside me, and I noticed that he shivered when Gerhardus mentioned Koos Steyn's child.

It was moonlight. All around us was the desert. Our wagons seemed very small and lonely; there was something about them that looked very mournful. The women and children put their arms round one another and wept a long while. Our kaffirs stood some distance away and watched us. My wife Sannie put her hand in mine, and I thought of the concentration camp. Poor woman, she had suffered much. And I knew that her thoughts were the same as my own: that after all it was perhaps better that our children should have died then than now.

We had got so far into the desert that we began telling one another that we must be near the end. Although we knew that German West was far away, and that in the way we had been travelling we had got little more than into the beginning of the Kalahari, yet we tried to tell one another lies about how near water was likely to be. But, of course, we told those lies only to one another. Each man in his own heart knew what the real truth was. And later on we even stopped telling one another lies about what a good chance we had of getting out alive. You can understand how badly things had gone with us when you know that we no longer troubled about hiding our position from the women and children. They wept, some of them. But that made no difference then. Nobody tried to comfort the women and children who cried. We knew that tears were useless, and yet somehow at that hour we felt that the weeping of the women was not less useless than the courage of the men. After a while there was no more weeping in our camp. Some of the women who lived through the dreadful things of the days that came after, and got safely back to the Transvaal, never again wept. What they had seen appeared to have hardened them. In this respect they had become as men. I think that is the saddest thing that ever happens in this world, when women pass through great suffering that makes them become as men.

That night we hardly slept. Early the next morning the men went out to look for water. An hour after sun-up Ferreira came back and told us that he had found a muddy pool a few miles away. We all went there, but there wasn't much water. Still, we got a little, and that made us feel better. It was only when it came to driving our cattle towards the mud-hole that we found our kaffirs had deserted us during the night. After we had gone to sleep they had stolen away. Some of the weaker cattle couldn't get up to go to the pool. So we left them. Some were trampled to death or got choked in the mud, and we had to pull them out to let the rest get to the hole. It was pitiful.

Just before we left one of Ferreira's daughters died. We scooped a hole in the sand and buried her.

So we decided to trek back.

After his daughter was dead Abraham Ferreira went up to Gerhardus and told him that if we had taken his advice earlier on and gone back, his daughter would not have died.

"Your daughter is dead now, Abraham," Gerhardus said. "It is no use talking about her any longer. We all have to die some day. I refused to go back earlier. I have decided to go back now."

Abraham Ferreira looked Gerhardus in the eyes and laughed. I shall always remember how that laughter sounded in the desert. In Abraham's voice there was the hoarseness of the sand and thirst. His voice was cracked with what the desert had done to him; his face was lined and his lips were blackened. But there was nothing about him that spoke of grief for his daughter's death.

"Your daughter is still alive, Oom Gerhardus," Abraham Ferreira said, pointing to the wagon wherein lay Gerhardus's wife, who was weak, and the child to whom she had given birth only a few months before. "Yes, she is still alive. . . so far."

Ferreira turned away laughing, and we heard him a little later explaining to his wife in cracked tones about the joke he had made.

Gerhardus Grobbelaar merely watched the other man walk away without saying anything. So far we had followed Gerhardus through all things, and our faith in him had been great. But now that we had decided to trek back we lost our belief in him. We lost it suddenly, too. We knew that it was best to turn back, and that to continue would mean that we would all die in the Kalahari. And yet, if Gerhardus had said we must still go on we would have done so. We would have gone through with him right to the end. But now that he as much as said he was beaten by the desert we had no more faith in Gerhardus. That is why I have said that Paul Kruger was a greater man than Gerhardus. Because Paul Kruger was that kind of man whom we still worshipped even when he decided to retreat. If it had been Paul Kruger who told us that we had to go back we would have returned with strong hearts. We would have retained exactly the same love for our leader, even if we knew that he was beaten. But from the moment that Gerhardus said we must go back we all knew that he was no longer our leader. Gerhardus knew that also.

We knew what lay between us and Malopolole and there was grave doubt in our hearts when we turned our wagons round. Our cattle were very weak, and we had to inspan all that could walk. We hadn't enough yokes, and therefore we cut poles from the scattered bushes and tied them to the trek-chains. As we were also without skeis we had to fasten the necks of the oxen straight on to the yokes with strops, and several of the oxen got strangled.

Then we saw that Koos Steyn had become mad. For he refused to return. He inspanned his oxen and got ready to trek on. His wife sat silent in the wagon with the baby; wherever her husband went she would go, too. That was only right, of course. Some women kissed her goodbye, and cried. But Koos Steyn's wife did not cry. We reasoned with Koos about it, but he said that he had made up his mind to cross the Kalahari, and he was not going to turn back just for nonsense.

"But, man," Gerhardus Grobbelaar said to him, "you've got no water to drink."

"I'll drink coffee then," Koos Steyn answered, laughing as always, and took up the whip and walked away beside the wagon. And Webber went off with him, just because Koos Steyn had been good to him, I suppose. That's why I have said that Englishmen are queer. Webber must have known that if Koos Steyn had not actually gone wrong in the head, still what he was doing now was madness, and yet he stayed with him.

We separated. Our wagons went slowly back to Malopolole. Koos Steyn's wagon went deeper into the desert. My wagon went last. I looked back at the Steyns. At that moment Webber also looked round. He saw me and waved his hand. It reminded me of that day in the Boer War when that other Englishman, whose companion we had shot, also turned round and waved.

Eventually we got back to Malopolole with two wagons and a handful of cattle. We abandoned the other wagons. Awful things happened on that desert. A number of children died. Gerhardus Grobbelaar's wagon was in front of me. Once I saw a bundle being dropped through the side of the wagon-tent. I knew what it was. Gerhardus would not trouble to bury his dead child, and his wife lay in the tent too weak to move. So I got off the wagon and scraped a small heap of sand over the body. All I remember of the rest of the journey to Malopolole is the sun and the sand. And the thirst. Although at one time we thought that we had lost our way, yet that did not matter much to us. We were past feeling. We could neither pray nor curse, our parched tongues cleaving to the roofs of our mouths.

Until today I am not sure how many days we were on our way back, unless I sit down and work it all out, and then I suppose I get it wrong. We got back to Malopolole and water. We said we would never go away from there again. I don't think that even those parents who had lost children grieved about them then. They were stunned with what they had gone through. But I knew that later on it would all come back again. Then they would remember things about shallow graves in the sand, and Gerhardus Grobbelaar and his wife would think of a little bundle lying out in the Kalahari. And I knew how they would feel.

Afterwards we fitted out a wagon with fresh oxen; we took an abundant supply of water and went back into the desert to look for the Steyn family. With the help of the Sechuana kaffirs, who could see tracks that we could not see, we found the wagon. The oxen had been outspanned; a few lay dead beside the wagon. The kaffirs pointed out to us footprints on the sand, which showed which way those two men and that woman had gone.

In the end we found them.

Koos Steyn and his wife lay side by side in the sand; the woman's head rested on the man's shoulder; her long hair had become loosened, and blew about softly in the wind. A great deal of fine sand had drifted over their bodies. Near them the Englishman lay, face downwards. We never found the baby Jemima. She must have died somewhere along the way and Koos Steyn must have buried her. But we agreed that the Englishman Webber must have passed through terrible things; he could not even have had any understanding left as to what the Steyns had done with their baby. He probably thought, up to the moment when he died, that he was carrying the child. For, when we lifted his body, we found, still clasped in his dead and rigid arms, a few old rags and a child's clothes.

It seemed to us that the wind that always stirs in the Kalahari blew very quietly and softly that morning.

Yes, the wind blew very gently.

Splendours from Ramoutsa

N o – Oom Schalk Lourens said – no, I don't know why it is that people always ask me to tell them stories. Even though they all know that I can tell better stories than anybody else. Much better. What I mean is, I wonder why people listen to stories. Of course, it is easy to understand why a man should ask me to tell him a story when there is drought in the Marico. Because then he can sit on the stoep and smoke his pipe and drink coffee, while I am talking, so that my story keeps him from having to go to the borehole, in the hot sun, to pump water for his cattle.

By the earnest manner in which the farmers of the Marico ask me for stories at certain periods, I am always able to tell that there is no breeze to drive the windmill, and the pump-handle is heavy, and the water is very far down. And at such times I have often observed the look of sorrow that comes into a man's eyes, when he knows that I am near the end of my story and that he will shortly have to reach for his hat.

And when I have finished the story he says, "Yes, Oom Schalk. That is the way of the world. Yes, that story is very deep."

But I know that all the time he is really thinking of how deep the water is in the borehole.

As I have said, it is when people have other reasons for asking me to tell them a story that I start wondering as I do now. When they ask me at those times when there is no ploughing to be done and there are no barbed-wire fences to be put up in the heat of the day. And I think that these reasons are deeper than any stories and deeper than the water in the boreholes when there is drought.

There was young Krisjan Geel, for instance. He once listened to a story. It was foolish of him to have listened, of course, especially as I hadn't told it to him. He had heard it from the Indian behind the counter of the shop in Ramoutsa. Krisjan Geel related this story to me, and I told him straight out that I didn't think much of it. I said anybody could guess, right from the start, why the princess was sitting beside the well. Anybody could see that she hadn't come there just because she was thirsty. I also said that the story was too long, and that even if I was thinking of something else I would still have told it in such a way

139

that people would have wanted to hear it to the end. I pointed out lots of other details like that.

Krisjan Geel said he had no doubt that I was right, but that the man who told him the story was only an Indian, after all, and that for an Indian, perhaps, it wasn't too bad. He also said that there were quite a number of customers in the place, and that made it more difficult for the Indian to tell the story properly, because he had to stand at such an awkward angle, all the time, weighing out things with his foot on the scale.

By his tone it sounded as though Krisjan Geel was quite sorry for the Indian.

So I spoke to him very firmly.

"The Indian in the store at Ramoutsa," I said, "has told me much better stories than that before today. He once told me that there were no burnt mealies mixed with the coffee-beans he sold me. Another one that was almost as good was when he said – "

"And to think that the princess went and waited by the well," Krisjan Geel interrupted me, "just because once she had seen the young man there."

" – Another good one," I insisted, "was when he said that there was no Kalahari sand in the sack of yellow sugar I bought from him."

"And she had only seen him once," Krisjan Geel went on, "and she was a princess."

" – And I had to give most of that sugar to the pigs," I said, "it didn't melt or sweeten the coffee. It just stayed like mud at the bottom of the cup."

"She waited by the well because she was in love with him," Krisjan Geel ended up, lamely.

" – I just mixed it in with the pigs' mealie-meal," I said, "they ate it very fast. It's funny how fast a pig eats."

Krisjan Geel didn't say any more after that one. No doubt he realised that I wasn't going to allow him to impress me with a story told by an Indian; and not very well told either. I could see what the Indian's idea was. Just because I had stopped buying from his shop after that unpleasantness about the coffee-beans and the sugar – which were only burnt mealies and Kalahari sand, as I explained to a number of my neighbours – he had hit on this uncalled-for way of paying me back. He was setting up as my rival. He was also going to tell stories.

And on account of the long start I had on him he was using all sorts of unfair methods. Like putting princesses in his stories. And palaces. And elephants that were all dressed up with yellow and red hangings and that were trained to trample on the king's enemies at the word of command. Whereas the only kind of elephants I could talk about were those that didn't wear red hangings or gold bangles and that didn't worry about whether or not you were the king's enemy: they just trampled on you first, anyhow, and without any sort of training either.

At first I felt it was very unfair of the Indian to come along with stories like that. I couldn't compete. And I began to think that there was much reason in what some of the speakers said at election meetings about the Indian problem.

But when I had thought it over carefully, I knew it didn't matter. The Indian could tell all the stories he wanted to about a princess riding around on an elephant. For there was one thing that I knew I could always do better than the Indian. Just in a few words, and without even talking about the princess, I would be able to let people know, subtly, what was in her heart. And this was more important than the palaces and the temples and the elephants with gold ornaments on their feet.

Perhaps the Indian realised the truth of what I am saying now. At all events, after a while he stopped wasting the time of his customers with stories of emperors. In between telling them that the price of sheep-dip and axle-grease had gone up. Or perhaps his customers got tired of listening to him.

But before that happened several of the farmers had hinted to me, in what they thought was a pleasantly amusing manner, that I would have to start putting more excitement into my stories if I wanted to keep in the fashion. They said I would have to bring in at least a king and a couple of princes, somehow, and also a string of elephants with Namaqualand diamonds in their ears.

I said they were talking very foolishly. I pointed out that there was no sense in my trying to tell people about kings and princes and trained elephants, and so on, when I didn't know anything about them or what they were supposed to do even.

"They don't need to do anything," Frik Snyman explained, "you can just mention that there was a procession like that nearby when whatever you are talking about happened. You can just mention them quickly, Oom Schalk, and you needn't say anything about them until you are in the middle of your next story. You can explain that the people in the procession had nothing to do with the story, because they were only passing through to some other place."

Of course, I said that that was nonsense. I said that if I had to keep on using that same procession over and over again, the people in it would be very travel-stained after they had passed through a number of stories. It would be a ragged and dust-laden procession.

"And the next time you tell us about a girl going to Nagmaal in Zeerust, Oom Schalk," Frik Snyman went on, "you can say that two men held up a red umbrella for her and that she had jewels in her hair, and she was doing a snake-dance."

I knew that Frik Snyman was only speaking like that, thoughtlessly, because of things he had seen in the bioscope that had gone to his head.

Nevertheless, I had to listen to many unreasonable remarks of this description before the Indian at Ramoutsa gave up trying to entertain his customers with empty discourse.

The days passed, and the drought came, and the farmers of the Marico put in much of their time at the boreholes, pushing the heavy pump-handles up and down. So that the Indian's brief period of story-telling was almost forgotten. Even Krisjan Geel came to admit that there was such a thing as overdoing these stories of magnificence.

"All these things he says about temples, and so on," Krisjan Geel said, "with white floors and shining red stones in them. And rajahs. Do you know what a rajah is, Oom Schalk? No, I don't know, either. You can have too much of that. It was only that one story of his that was any good. That one about the princess. She had rich stones in her hair, and pearls sewn on to her dress. And so the young man never guessed why she had come there. He didn't guess that she loved him. But perhaps I didn't tell you the story properly the first time, Oom Schalk. Perhaps I should just tell it to you again. I have already told it to many people."

But I declined his offer hurriedly. I replied that there was no need for him to go over all that again. I said that I remembered the story very well and that if it was all the same to him I should prefer not to hear it a second time. He might just spoil it in telling it again.

But it was only because he was young and inexperienced, I said, that he had allowed the Indian's story to carry him away like that. I told him about other young men whom I had known at various times, in the Marico, who had formed wrong judgments about things and who had afterwards come along and told me so.

"Why you are so interested in that story," I said, "is because you like to imagine yourself as that young man."

Krisjan Geel agreed with me that this was the reason why the Indian's story had appealed to him so much. And he went on to say that a young man had no chance, really, in the Marico. What with the droughts, and the cattle getting the miltsiek, and the mosquitoes buzzing around so that you couldn't sleep at night.

And when Krisjan Geel left me I could see, very clearly, how much he envied the young man in the Indian's story.

As I have said before, there are some strange things about stories and about people who listen to them. I thought so particularly on a hot afternoon, a few weeks later, when I saw Lettie Viljoen. The sun shone on her upturned face and on her bright yellow hair. She sat with one hand pressed in the dry grass of last summer, and I thought of what a graceful figure she was, and of how slender her wrists were.

And because Lettie Viljoen hadn't come there riding on an elephant with orange trappings and gold bangles, and because she wasn't wearing a string of red stones at her throat, Krisjan Geel knew, of course, that she wasn't a princess.

And I suppose that this was the reason why, during all the time in which he was talking to her, telling her that story about the princess at the well, Krisjan Geel never guessed about Lettie Viljoen, and what it was that had brought her there, in the heat of the sun, to the borehole.

Notes on the Text

THE textual history of *Mafeking Road* is a complicated one. The twenty-one stories that make up the collection were all first published individually between 1930 and 1946 – in the first issues of *The Touleier* and then in the weekly *The South African Opinion* during the 1930s, and in its successor, the monthly *The S. A. Opinion*, in the 1940s, where ten of them were reprinted as well (see the listing below). The problems began when these stories were compiled by Bosman into the first edition of *Mafeking Road*.

The correspondence between Bosman and Roy Campbell quoted in the introduction offers some clues as to what must have occurred when Bosman was unexpectedly approached by the CNA to prepare the volume. When he collected together "such stories as [he] could lay [his] hands on" (as he remarked to Campbell) he turned hurriedly to the published copies of them in *The Touleier* and *The S. A. Opinion.* He probably extracted the relevant pages from these periodicals, preferring where applicable a later version of any story which he had revised quite recently for reprinting. There was never any question of an original manuscript or typescript source – presumably they were all long lost. This is what in his "Talk of the Town" column of November, 1946, in *The S. A. Opinion*, on which he now served as literary editor, he described as blandly as follows: "I was engaged for a couple of days last week in going through old files of newspapers and magazines, making a collection of stories which I had written over the past fifteen years." A year later *Mafeking Road* would be out in hardback.

In this way Bosman assembled the bundle of texts from which the original edition of *Mafeking Road* was set. This reconstruction of events is corroborated by a letter written by his stalwart publisher, William Wolpert, Deputy General Manager of the CNA, to Helena Lake, Bosman's widow and copyright-holder, in June, 1960, responding to her query regarding the possible existence of some manuscript of *Mafeking Road*. Wolpert frankly replied: "I cannot find the original MS of 'Mafeking Road' and as far as I can remember the material all came from the stories which were printed in South African periodicals."

Bosman's haste, the lack of accurate reprographic technology, poor copy-editing, the amateurish state of some South African book production at the time: these factors all led to *Mafeking Road* first appearing in the condition Bosman described to Campbell. The situation has not improved since. Mistakes that were initially embedded in the 1947 edition were seriously compounded when it came to the reset 1949 Dassie edition. By then – and Bosman was still alive to notice this – nearly a hundred errors had been introduced. Little wonder he was aggrieved and so desperate to find an overseas publisher, which would have afforded him the opportunity of having the collection reset from scratch. A professional proofreader himself, of course his aggravation was extreme.

But the process of corruption was destined to continue. Generations of copy-editors since his death have indeed attempted to tidy up the book, but as it turns out have only introduced yet further slips and inconsistencies. There have been no fewer than three resettings of *Mafeking Road* since 1949 for various editions, but there is no evidence that any systematic attempt has been made to fulfil the author's desire "to restore [the stories] as far as possible to the way they were originally." No one, it appears, has yet gone back to the original stories to produce a reliable edition of *Mafeking Road*.

Here I have attempted to reconstruct the text that Bosman himself must have compiled, by returning to the versions of the stories originally published in South African periodicals in the 1930s and 40s, all kept safely in the reference section of the Central Library of the Greater Johannesburg Library Services (or the Johannesburg Public Library, as it used to be called, and which Bosman himself praised often enough). The copy-text that has been used for each story is the version that originally appeared, or (in the case of ten of the stories) the version subsequently republished under Bosman's own editorial control.

Obviously these versions, although closely supervised by Bosman or by his friends and associates, were themselves not entirely immune to errors. Also, over the lengthy timespan of the sixteen years that went into this cross-section of the Oom Schalk venture, spelling, typographical and other conventions changed. Inconsistencies have had to be rectified in the normal copy-editing way: the problem of choosing krantz, instead of krans or *krantz*, and sticking with it; and of allowing Oom Schalk to keep saying "I wish I did not do that" in his own dialect.

However, it was the *introduction* of errors into the editions of *Mafeking Road* in 1947 and 1949 that so riled Bosman. In most cases these were more serious than printers' blips. He felt that unseen hands had tampered with the meaning of the stories against his wishes, often to the extent of censoring them; certainly blurring his intentions.

A few examples will have to suffice. The story most affected by the changes – and the one the "mutilated form" of which no doubt most irked Bosman – is the largest of them here, his early masterpiece "The Rooinek." As in most other instances, the 1949 Dassie version is the most corrupt: there two whole sentences were omitted and one changed significantly; six individual words were also omitted and one erroneously introduced; and seven new errors of punctuation were added. When Bosman noticed that pieces of stories "were cut as if for reasons of space", he no doubt had this one in mind.

These cuts have meant that the reader has been unaware up to now that Oom Schalk is certain of hitting the Englishman who gets off his horse to rescue his wounded comrade in the opening passages of the story. The sentence "At that distance I couldn't miss" has always been dropped, and the Englishman's astounding courage thus downplayed. When in the same story the families which have embarked on the trek across the Kalahari kneel down in prayer, what is foremost in the Englishman's mind is the fate of, not himself, but Koos Steyn's child ("The Englishman knelt down beside me, and I noticed that he shivered when Gerhardus mentioned Koos Steyn's child" has been omitted). At the end, when the party returns to search for Koos Steyn and his family, it is the Englishman's presence among the corpses that is pointedly stressed ("Near them the Englishman lay, face downwards" has been lost). Such lacunae have meant that the outstanding qualities of this Englishman (bravery, loyalty) came to be underplayed. Important nuances have simply gone missing.

Similar errors occur in "The Widow", where two sentences came to be omitted. In this case, however, there is a ready explanation. The layout artist of the September, 1946 *S.A. Opinion* version, evidently running out of space, introduced a cut at the bottom of one column and another at the end of a page. In both cases the cuts produced garbled sentences ("They said it was impossible for her to continue in this way, with that if she did not break down and weep she could not go on living much longer"; "A small group had gathered at the Among the spectators was Francina Theron, looking very frail and slender in her widow's weeds"). A later copy-editor or typesetter attempted to solve the first problem by changing "with" to "and": "They said it was impossible for her to continue in this way, and that if she did not break down. . . " Solving the second problem appeared to require the introduction of "courthouse" followed by a period: "A small group had gathered at the courthouse. Among the spectators. . . " Had the earlier (April, 1935) *South African Opinion* version of the story been consulted, the passages would have been restored as follows (the italics indicate the omitted fragments): "They said it was impossible for her to continue in this way, with *that stony grief inside her. They said* that if she did not break down. . . "; "A small group had gathered at the *graveside. Some were kneeling in prayer*. Among the spectators was Francina Theron. . . " Needless to say, these references to Francina Theron's "stony grief", to the "graveside" (instead of "courthouse"), and to people "kneeling in prayer" add subtle, important effects to a close reading of the story.

These are examples of the more substantive errors in earlier editions, but there are many others of a minor (although no less irritating) nature. In the March, 1944 *S. A. Opinion* version of "Starlight on the Veld" there is evidence that the last passages were condensed in order to fit into the space available: one paragraph break was ignored, and two words and one comma simply deleted. Again, the earlier *South African Opinion* version of the story would have assisted later editors here. So, when the romantic Jan Ockerse expresses the feeling he has for the stars (which he associates with a long-lost love), it is appropriate – and stylistically more felicitous – that he should repeat "very": "The lower one of those three stars – ah, it has just faded – is very near to me. Yes, it is very near" instead of the truncated "The lower of those three stars – ah, it has just faded – is very near to me. Yes, it is near."

Some of the errors are simple word-substitutions that were then slavishly carried through from one edition to another. In the October, 1935 *South African Opinion* version of "Marico Scandal" Francina Deventer, who is still in love with Gawie (despite his being shunned by the community for reputedly having a touch of the tar), looks at her father "in a disapproving sort of way" when she thinks that he has made an unflattering remark about Gawie. This erroneously (and pointlessly) becomes "disappointing sort of way" in the September, 1944 *S. A. Opinion* version, is then "corrected" in the 1947 edition of

Mafeking Road as "disappointed sort of way", and is carried thus through every subsequent edition. Similar errors occur in almost all of the stories: "range" instead of "rante", "the" instead of "their", "places" instead of "palaces", "lamp" instead of "light", "also" instead of "all so". . . the list goes on and on.

Other interesting points emerge from a close examination of the early versions of the stories. The very first published Oom Schalk story, "Makapan's Caves" (1930), used inverted commas throughout to denote Oom Schalk's speaking voice. This clumsy device was soon dropped as Bosman streamlined his style. Other evolutionary changes occurred. Words like "veldskoen" and "aasvoël", which were italicised in early stories, later became naturalised and rendered in regular type. Of course, the use of italics to denote the 'foreignness' of Afrikaans words is distinctly anomalous in that Oom Schalk was ostensibly speaking Afrikaans and would hardly enunciate "veldskoen" with a special inflection. And the illusion that he is *speaking* (not writing) had also to be maintained – hence Oom Schalk's propensity for short, mostly monosyllabic words (around four letters per word, on average).

Significant cuts were made by Bosman himself to three of the stories when he reprinted them in the new series of *S. A. Opinion*, and it is these later versions as representing his last texts that have gone into all editions of *Mafeking Road* (including the present one). In two cases – "Yellow Moepels" and "The Music Maker" – large chunks of text were excised, presumably in the interests of conciseness. The loss of most of these passages has indeed been a gain in terms of tautness of narrative structure. However, some wonderfully funny moments have also been irretrievably lost to readers of *Mafeking Road*.

One of these occurs in "Yellow Moepels", the story about the ill-fated love affair between Schalk's friend and comrade-in-arms, Neels Potgieter, and Martha Rossouw, the woman who no longer wants him when he returns from war to the ripening moepels. In a characteristic digression about men's unreliable recollections of their war experiences, in the original version Oom Schalk recounted the case of Klaas Uys:

Once, in my presence, Klaas Uys told an Englishman about the fighting he had done.

"Do you remember the Battle of – ?" the Englishman asked him, afterwards, mentioning a foreign place that I had never heard of before – and that I am sure Klaas hadn't heard of, either. But you couldn't trap Klaas Uys as easily as all that.

"Oh, yes," he answered, "I fought right through it. I shot seventeen red-coats in the tambookie grass."

"And Wellington?" the Englishman asked, "did you see him?"

"I fired at him twice," Klaas Uys admitted, "but I missed him. He ran away so fast through the mealie-lands."

The Englishman did not answer. He looked very far out across the veld. I suppose he was thinking about how fine it must be to belong to a nation that could produce as fearless a fighting-man as Klaas Uys.

This part of the story in *Mafeking Road* is also very funny, but the long excursus about Klaas Uys is reduced to a single paragraph: "Klaas Uys was a man like that. Each year, on his birthday, he remembered one or two more redcoats that he had shot, whereupon he got up straight away and put another few notches in the wood part of his rifle, along the barrel. And he said his memory was getting better every year."

The cuts made to the original version of "The Music Maker" are a loss in the same way. When Manie Kruger the concertina-player declares that if he wanted to get into history he would have to die of consumption in the arms of a princess, Jan Terreblanche used to retort: "Perhaps it would be better if you died of snake-bite. . . It's so much quicker. Or of the pig measles." And Oom Schalk observed in his poker-faced manner: "But then Jan Terreblanche was that kind of man. He was very good at jacking up a wagon that had got stuck in the mud, or at making biltong, but he had very little of what you can call the finer feelings about life."

Another passage cut from this story shows Oom Schalk to be less of an old racist than he is usually taken to be. When he describes Manie Kruger's "recitals", which he calls "very impressive", he goes on to remark: "Nevertheless, there was also a certain amount of unpleasantness about them." Part of this "unpleasantness", we later discover, is when there is trouble with the green curtain that Manie so incongruously uses and he gets up to "kick the kaffir." Oom Schalk previously remarked at this point: "That was another part of the unpleasantness that I have already mentioned to you." This was all dropped by Bosman in his later version. Although the story is the better for the cuts in this instance, it is interesting to see Oom Schalk showing disapproval of the abusive behaviour of one of his fellow Marico farmers.

A somewhat contrary instance occurs in "Brown Mamba", where Bosman cut the following reference to Bechuana unfamiliarity with white burials: "It was desirable to get a hymn with which the Bechuanas were also conversant. Hendrik questioned them to this end, eliciting the fact that their knowledge of sacred song was limited to a corrupt version of 'Yes, We Have No Bananas', which one of their number had brought back with him from the Johannesburg mines." As this is also the only story in *Mafeking Road* which does not use Oom Schalk as a narrator, perhaps it was too risky for Bosman himself to include such a passage and remain credible.

Indeed, the inclusion of "Brown Mamba" in *Mafeking Road* raises an interesting point about his principles of selection. At least a dozen other Oom Schalk stories were eligible in late 1946, including obvious ones like "The Wind in the Trees" and "Seed-time and Harvest" (both included in *Unto Dust* posthumously). Why select a non-Oom Schalk story in what is otherwise a cycle? One can only speculate on his reasons for this, but it is possible that, in throwing it together, Bosman did not give much attention to the question of the collection's internal coherence; perhaps he really did just use what came to hand.

But the issue here is by what principle the text of the present edition of *Mafeking Road* should be brought together. Why, it may be asked, have I not reverted to earlier versions of stories if they contain passages (like those quoted above) that add to our enjoyment and appreciation? And why not drop "Brown Mamba" and include another Oom Schalk story in the interests of continuity and logic? The answer in both cases is clear: this edition of *Mafeking Road* at last attempts to restore the stories as far as possible to the versions that we know were preferred by Bosman, and which he considered final. Clearly, this decision also includes treating his own selection and arrangement of them as inviolable.

Versions of stories used as copy-texts here (in order of first appearance). Reprints followed, where applicable:

1. "Makapan's Caves." *Touleier* 1.1 (Dec 1930): 15-20.
2. "The Rooinek" (Parts 1 and 2). *Touleier* 1.2 (Jan-Feb 1931): 8-13 and 1.3 (Mar 1931):126-132.
3. "The Gramophone." *Touleier* 1.5 (May 1931): 310-313.
4. "Veld Maiden." *SAO* 1.4 (14 Dec 1934): 9-10.

5. "Yellow Moepels." *SAO* 1.7 (25 Jan 1935): 7-8; reprinted *SAO* 2.2 (Apr 1945): 14-15.
6. "The Love Potion." *SAO* 1.9 (22 Feb 1935): 8-9.
7. "In the Withaak's Shade." *SAO* 1.11 (22 Mar 1935): 4-5; reprinted *SAO* 2.1 (Mar 1945): 18-19, 30.
8. "The Widow." *SAO* 1.13 (19 Apr 1935): 10-11; reprinted *SAO* 3.7 (Sept 1946): 14-15, 20.
9. "Brown Mamba." *SAO* 1.14 (3 May 1935): 8-9; reprinted *SAO* 2.6 (Aug 1945): 14-15, 30.
10. "Willem Prinsloo's Peach Brandy." *SAO* 1.15 (17 May 1935): 5-6.
11. "Ox-wagons on Trek." *SAO* 1.16 (31 May 1935): 6-7; reprinted *SAO* 2.12 (Feb 1946): 20-21, 30.
12. "The Music Maker." *SAO* 1.20 (26 July 1935): 6-7; reprinted *SAO* 2.7 (Sept 1945): 18-19.
13. "Drieka and the Moon." *SAO* 1.21 (9 Aug 1935): 8-9; reprinted *SAO* 3.2 (Apr 1946): 18-19, 21.
14. "The Mafeking Road." *SAO* 1.22 (23 Aug 1935): 6-7; reprinted *SAO* 1.10 (Dec 1944): 12-13, 28.
15. "Marico Scandal." *SAO* 1.25 (4 Oct 1935): 8-10; reprinted *SAO* 1.7 (Sept 1944): 18-19.
16. "Bechuana Interlude." *SAO* 1.26 (18 Oct 1935): 11-13.
17. "Starlight on the Veld." *SAO* 2.6 (10 Jan 1936): 9-11; reprinted *SAO* 1.1 (Mar 1944): 20-21, 31.
18. "Splendours from Ramoutsa." *SAO* 3.9 (20 Feb 1937): 9-10.
19. "Dream by the Bluegums." *SAO* 3.18 (26 June 1937): 12-13.
20. "The Prophet." *SAO* 2.10 (Dec 1945): 10-11, 31.
21. "Mampoer." *SAO* 2.11 (Jan 1946): 14-15, 27.